Do No Evil

—〰—

"Hear no evil . . . See no evil . . . Speak no evil . . . "
Now there's one more
evil to avoid.

Harold J. Fischel

Cover Design and Production by Angelheart Design

ISBN: 069269210X
ISBN 13: 9780692692103
Library of Congress Control Number: 2016906276
Moose & Buck Publishing, Chelsea, MI

I dedicate this novel to those who expose people who commit evil deeds while claiming to right the wrongs of the World.

The Author

My family fled the Netherlands shortly after the Nazi invasion. During that time most countries did not accept refugees and we passed through half a dozen countries before settling in Curacao and later in Aruba. We immigrated to the United States in 1952. I have lived and worked on four different continents.

I am a graduate of Washington & LeeUniversity and the NYU School of Law.

After law school I joined a law firm in New York City. At Washington and Lee I enrolled in the R.O.T.C program and was called to active duty in 1964. I served in the US Army in Germany, retiring as a captain after my tour of duty was completed. The Secretary of the Army awarded me The Army Commendation Medal for my service. I took an overseas discharged and lived and worked in the Netherlands for many years, before returning to the United States where I joined the US subsidiary of a Chinese company. I am retired now and live in Michigan with my wife, Jan. I have two daughters, five wonderful grandchildren, and two great sons-in-law. Since retiring, I have published four novels and am working on a fifth.

I

The noise was so loud that Jason heard it all the way up in his room on the third floor. At first he thought something big, like a car or a truck, had crashed into the house, but the banging continued. He got up from his desk and raced down two sets of stairs to see where the noise was coming from. As he bounced down the final few steps, he realized that someone was pounding on the front door. He raced to the door and jerked it open. Caroline was lying crouched up against the door, tears streaming down her face, her whole body shaking uncontrollably. Jason threw his arms around his girlfriend.

"Caroline, baby, what happened?"

Caroline grabbed onto Jason and held him so tightly he could hardly breathe. She tried to speak but the words seemed to stop in her throat. Jason thought he could hear her say, "He was going to rape me." He pushed his head gently against her wet cheek in an effort to comfort her.

He whispered softly in her ear, "Baby, my poor baby. It's going to be okay, I'm here. I won't let anybody hurt you."

Jason tried to pick her up and take her inside. Normally, at barely five foot eleven and with his slight build, he could not have lifted the big girl with her muscular, athletic body. But this time he managed to pick Caroline up and carry her into the living room where he laid her down on the large circular couch in front of the fireplace.

Once again he asked, "What happened? Who attacked you?"

Caroline, still holding tightly onto Jason, who was awkwardly bent over the couch, calmed down enough to tell Jason what had happened to her.

"Ever since Mom died he was making advances."

"Who is *he*?" Jason asked.

"James, my stepfather. He started making these inappropriate remarks soon after the accident that killed my mom. At first I thought his remarks were meant to make me feel good. To sort of indicate he was proud of me and would take care of me now Mom was gone."

Jason interrupted her, "What type of remarks? What exactly did he say?"

"Oh, things like, 'you look really nice in that sweater.' I now realize he was talking about my breasts. At times he would be glaring at my behind and comment about how nice my jeans fit. I really started worrying when he began to push me into joining him in drinking wine with our dinner. He usually would polish off a bottle by himself, even after having a few stiff drinks of whisky when he got home."

Again Jason interrupted her. "Why in the world didn't you tell me about this?"

"Oh, come on! Get serious. We're talking about James Olsen. *The* James Olson, president of the Bayville Mutual Bank, head of the school board of P. J. Richard Memorial High School; the famous James Olson whom my mother married almost a decade ago when I was barely seven years old. We're talking about my stepfather! How in the hell could I tell anyone, even you, that this man was making sexual advances toward me? I kept telling myself I was just imagining things. I refused to believe what his true intentions were. I kept convincing myself I was being silly and that he was just showing me he was proud of me and happy to be my stepfather.

"He always gave me everything I wanted. He bought me things I needed, or even things I didn't need, things I just wanted to have. My mom loved this man, and in a way, so did I. But tonight everything became clear. He was really pushy about drinking with him, even though I have repeatedly told him that because of Mom's accident, I'll never touch alcohol. You know she was drunk when she crashed into that tree. It really shook me up when he suggested we go into the hot tub together. But even then I refused to think anything bad about his suggestion. Mom and I used to get into the hot tub together all the time. I started to go to my room to put on a bathing suit when he said that would not be necessary. He smiled and called me a prude. He said that most people prefer being nude in the hot tub. I laughed that off and got up to go to my room to change into a bathing suit.

"When I passed his chair his hand not very accidently brushed against my breast. I could feel his fingers linger on my nipple. I quickly turned away but he very deliberately reached out and stroked my behind. I tried to stay calm and proceeded up the stairs to my room. I locked the door and called down to let him know I had a lot of homework and would pass on the hot tub. Moments later he knocked on my door. I did not open the door. I told him I had too much homework to take time out for the hot tub.

"He very forcefully told me to open the door and said we did not need the hot tub to show our affection for each other. He said, 'Let me in and I'll show you how much I love you.'

"I ran into my bathroom and into the other bedroom connected on the other side. From there I fled down the stairs and raced to my car. I had to get to you as quickly as possible. I knew I would be safe if I could get to you!"

II

Caroline and Jason were so involved in trying to figure out how to handle this situation that they did not hear Jason's mother enter the house. Mrs. Housten entered the living room just as Caroline said, "No, Jason, I don't want you to do that. You promised not to."

"Damn it, Jason, stop it. Leave the girl alone!" Caroline and Jason jumped up, frightened by the sudden interruption. They were confronted by a glaring Mrs. Housten, who was about to smack her son around the ears.

"Don't. Don't hit him! He did nothing wrong, it's not what you think."

"Then please tell me what the hell is going on between the two of you."

Caroline and Jason looked at each other, clearly confused as to what to say. Caroline awkwardly motioned with her hands to indicate that Jason should say something. Jason was at a loss as to what to tell his mother. He had just promised Caroline he would not tell anyone that her stepfather had sexually accosted her.

"I'm waiting for an explanation. What was happening just before I came home? Jason, you promised to respect Caroline. She is not that type of girl and you know it! You disgust me; trying something against her will."

It was Caroline who spoke up first. Mrs. Housten could tell she was indignant and her voice made it clear she was hurt by the way Mrs. Housten had spoken to her son.

"Mrs. Housten, Jason did nothing improper. You know very well that during all the time he and I have been going together he has never done anything improper. Jason would never do anything against my will. You know that!"

"Yes, I have always believed that, and I apologize for my reaction and for what I said. I guess I have become a little overly protective of you, Caroline. Of course I trust my son. But over the years I have come to consider you as more than just another of Jason's girlfriends. I sense that something bad has happened. Please trust me and share with me what happened. You know I love you both and I'll protect you, no matter what happened."

Jason looked at Caroline. He knew he could not break his promise to her; he could not be the one to tell his mother about Caroline's stepfather. To his relief, he was not put into that position.

With a loud shriek, Caroline threw herself into the arms of Mrs. Housten. Between sobs she tried to explain to Jason's mom, "I had to get to Jason. I needed him to protect me; I know that man would have raped me if I hadn't gotten away. I had to get to Jason; I knew I would be safe if I could get to your house."

"Oh my God, you poor child! What man? Did he touch you? Are you hurt? Do I know who attacked you?" Caroline did not answer; she kept on crying and attempted to gain comfort by digging deeper into the arms and chest of Mrs. Housten. Mrs. Housten responded by yelling at Jason, "Make hot tea for her. Quick, get me a blanket, she is going into shock; we must keep her warm. No, no, first call the police!"

Hearing Mrs. Housten call for the police got an instant reaction from Caroline. With tears still streaming down her face she begged Mrs. Housten not to involve the police. When Mrs. Housten balked at that, Caroline relented and started telling Mrs. Housten about her stepfather.

"But, dear child, we must call the police. We can't let him get away with that. We have to call the police!"

"Please, Mrs. Housten, please don't. I know my mom was not perfect and you didn't much care for her. But she was my mom and I loved her. Don't tarnish her memory any further by letting people know her husband went after her daughter. People already say too much about her drinking. Please, Mrs. Housten, keep what happened between us."

"I don't know if I legally can. I have to think about that. I may have a duty to report that pervert."

"He'll probably turn the whole thing around. He'll claim it was I who went after him. It will be his word against mine and they'll most likely believe him. He's the respected bank president, and I'm a nobody."

"You are not a nobody! Don't say that about yourself; you mean a lot to us. Don't worry, you won't have to go through the spectacle of a public trial. I would never put you in a position like that. But you can't go back to that house. I will not allow that."

"I don't want to go back. I'm afraid of him. But all my stuff is in his house; where would I stay if I don't go back? I can't go out and rent an apartment someplace; he'll never give me the money for that."

"That problem is easily solved. You'll move into my house. After my divorce from Jason's father I moved into this monstrously big house, which I inherited from my parents. Finally I'll have some use for at least one of those extra bedrooms."

"What if he tries to force me to move back? He is my stepfather and I'm not eighteen yet."

"Did he formally adopt you?"

"Don't think so."

"Then leave it to me, I'll take care of it. When I moved here to Bayville, Illinois, Jason's father moved his head office from New York to Chicago to be closer to his son. So he is close enough to help if we need him."

Mrs. Housten wanted to make a call without Caroline and Jason listening in. "You two go to the kitchen. Make some coffee or tea. We have to sit down and calm down so we can digest all this commotion. I'll join you in a few minutes; I have a few calls to make. Don't worry, I am not calling the police or any other authority. I think I can handle this without getting more people involved."

After Caroline and Jason had left the room, Mrs. Housten picked up the phone and dialed James Olson's house. She knew the number by heart from having dialed it so often in the past to invite Caroline to come over for dinner. The phone rang only twice before James picked up. Without first asking who was calling, James barked into the phone, "Caroline, you come home right now. I won't stand for your running out like that!"

"Sorry, James, it's not Caroline. It's Kitty Housten calling."

"Oh, sorry about that. How are you, Kitty? As you heard I'm having a little trouble with Caroline; you know how difficult teenagers can be."

"Actually, I know a lot. And I know that it's Caroline who has difficulties with you and not the other way around."

"What are you talking about? Has that brat been telling stories again?"

"James, just shut up and listen to what I have to say. If you want to hang up go ahead. I'll be over with the police, and you'll regret not hearing me out. I know exactly what you did to Caroline this evening. You can try to deny it, but that will not help you. I won't believe you. I now know what type of a man you are. You tried to take advantage of that dear girl, and I will stop you from ever coming near her again. You are a filthy predator and you will stay away from Caroline!

If you try to fight me on this, let me warn you. You'll not only be fighting me, Kitty Housten, but you'll have the full force of a very powerful man coming down on you. A local bank president is no match for the billionaire industrialist named Noah Housten. My ex-husband and I might not agree on many things, but if there is one thing we do agree on it is that Caroline is a lovely girl and our son Jason is lucky to have a wonderful girlfriend like her."

It was deathly silent on the other side of the line, but Kitty knew James had not hung up. So she continued. "Tomorrow after school, Caroline and I will come to your house. You will not be in the house or anywhere near. We will pack all her clothes and take them to my house. We will also pack and set aside any personal items she wishes to keep. You will not interfere when these items are picked up by professional movers in the next few days. Caroline will mail you her keys to the house after the last of her personal possessions are removed. I know her car is in her name but I'll take over the insurance. When all this is done I will receive a notarized document from you stating that you fully agree with Caroline's wish to live at my house and that you will not interfere with any and all arrangements I make on Caroline's behalf." Kitty took a deep breath before she continued.

"James, I don't think there have been incidents like this in the past with other girls or women. I'll give you the benefit of the doubt and treat it like an isolated incident. But let me assure you, if I ever hear about anything like this involving you, I'll come after you. This is a small town, and I'll know. I won't go so far as to say you could have been the cause of Caroline's mother drinking too much in the last couple of years of her life. That doesn't mean it hasn't crossed my mind. The only thing good you did tonight was not hanging up on me."

In a symbolic gesture, Kitty wiped off the receiver before she hung up. "I actually did it," she mumbled. "That was not at all like me. I must really like that girl. *Like* is not strong enough; I love her like a daughter." With that she got up and went to join Caroline and Jason in the kitchen.

A few days later day, when the three of them sat down for breakfast, Kitty admonished Jason. "Now that Caroline is living here with us you have to treat her like a sister rather than your girlfriend. This will be a strict rule while you're in the house, and if I ever catch you in her bedroom without me present, you'll regret it."

Jason responded with a curt, "Yes, Mom."

But after Caroline excused herself and went up to her new room to get ready for school, he sarcastically said, "Thanks for trusting me."

Before Kitty could respond he angrily threw out, "What am I? Some kind of sex maniac? Or even better, your son the rapist!"

"I'm sorry, son. My warning was probably uncalled for, and you did not deserve that. Again, I'm sorry if I hurt your feelings, but you have to appreciate that I have taken on a huge responsibility. I have never had a daughter, and now I'm responsible for this wonderful teenage girl. You're so lucky to have a girlfriend like that. But while she lives here, I will treat her like the daughter I never had. I want her to feel safe here. She should never feel she can stay here only as long as she is your girlfriend. That if, in the very unlikely case you make inappropriate overtures and she rejects you, she could jeopardize staying here.

"Jason, I trust you and I know you'll never do anything like her stepfather did. But that is not the point. During the past few years I have come to understand that it is more than puppy love between the two of you, but I just want Caroline to know she has no obligation to please you. I hope you understand how I feel."

Jason got up and gave Kitty a huge hug. "I am lucky as hell to have a great girlfriend, and I didn't do badly on the mom front either. I love you. I have said this before but I want to repeat it; it's fabulous that you have taken Caroline into your house and offered her a home here with us. You're the best! I don't understand how Dad could have left you."

"HUSH! You know very well I don't tolerate any negative talk about your father. We had our reasons for going our separate ways, and that is all you have to know. Your father is a genius who has built a large industrial empire from which you and I have been picking the fruits. I expect you to show him the respect he deserves."

"Mom, I was only trying to pay you a compliment. Besides, I hardly know my father."

"Jason, don't exaggerate. True, he doesn't live with us, but he has done his best to be part of your life. He even moved to Chicago to be near to you. Now go upstairs and get ready for school."

III

The news that Caroline was now living with Jason and his mom spread quickly. Like Kitty said, it's a small town. The usual suspects made a big deal out of it. Kitty was shocked and hurt to hear the off-color remarks about Jason and Caroline living together. She quickly set out to quell all rumors. Rather than say anything, she made a deliberate effort to be seen in town as much as possible with Caroline. The two of them could be seen shopping together almost on a daily basis. She even went so far as to drag Caroline along when she went to visit friends, and to meetings of her garden and book clubs. Before long, it became normal for Caroline to be living at her house.

She told Caroline to stop addressing her so formally with Mrs. Housten. "Just call me Kitty."

Caroline responded with, "I would love to call you Mom, would that be all right?"

Kitty had tears in her eyes when she responded, "That is so sweet of you. Yes, that would make me very happy. I would consider it an honor."

During the summer before their senior year, Caroline and Jason decided to go to college together. They researched the colleges that would be best for each of them and settled on Syracuse. Jason was a shoo-in to graduate as valedictorian of their class, and Caroline, a three-sport standout, had been selected as captain of the girl's field hockey team. They never really doubted they would be accepted, but when each of them got the letter of acceptance on the same day they decided to give a huge party to celebrate.

But somewhere along the way, things changed as far as Jason was concerned. One evening while they were doing their homework in the den, Jason said, "Caroline, I have been wanting to tell you something."

"What's up, honey? You sound so serious, is something wrong?"

"Nah, nothing is really wrong. But during the last year I have decided I want to study electronics. I love physics and that sort of stuff and I think I can develop important things in the electronics field."

"What's wrong with that? That's not a problem. I know you'll be great at it. Why so serious? You look like you're about to tell me one of our friends has died or something terrible like that."

"No, it's nothing like that. It's just that I decided Syracuse is not the right school for me. I went ahead and applied to MIT and Stanford."

"You what? You applied there and never told me?" Caroline sounded more hurt than angry.

"I knew you would be upset. So, in case I was not accepted by either school, I just wanted to keep it to myself."

"Keep it to yourself? We always discuss everything! I thought we had no secrets between us. Now you tell me you did not want to discuss something as important as this?"

"Calm down, it's not that way. I told you I was not sure I would be accepted, and then there would have been no need to bring up the subject."

"You really don't understand our relationship, do you?"

"Stop! Don't go there. Because of everything we planned, I did not know how to tell you I really did not want to go to Syracuse. You were so excited about it that I did not know how to bring up the subject. But now I have been accepted by both schools."

"Of course they accepted you! You're a fucking genius; you can get into any school you want." As she said it, Caroline calmed down. The fact that Jason had been accepted to two top schools sank in. "My God, Jason, you have been accepted to both MIT and Stanford! I don't think anyone from P. J. Richard Memorial High School has even come close to getting accepted to either. Come here; let me give you a big hug. That is huge! Wait till your father hears about that. That will make him sit up and take notice."

"So you don't mind if I don't go to Syracuse with you?"

"I'm devastated and thrilled all at the same time. I don't know how I'll go to Syracuse without you.

We've been together since the summer before our sophomore year. I can't really imagine being away from you. But what girl could begrudge the guy she loves being accepted to not one, but two, of the country's top schools? Give me a moment to recover while I cry my eyes out because I have to go to college without you, while gloating over the fact my love, my soul mate, is a genius."

Jason seemed to only hear the part in which Caroline expressed her pride in the fact that he had been accepted by two top schools. He never really tried to understand her sadness about not going to Syracuse together. The next morning, he did not even notice that Caroline had applied extra makeup to hide the fact that she had been crying for most of the night.

IV

Reggie McLaughlin and Jose Alvares were having lunch at Doc's when the conversation turned to an article Reggie had read about Jason in the on-line edition of the *New York Post*. "The SOB is back in the news again."

Reggie's remark surprised Jose. "Nice way to talk about your friend. The guy practically dragged you through high school. If I remember correctly, you would have been academically ineligible to play football if he hadn't spent hours tutoring you. Pumping all that stuff into your fat head was no mean feat. You would never have gotten that football scholarship at Michigan if he hadn't been willing to help you all through high school. And now you're calling him a SOB? It wasn't his fault that you flunked out after the first year. You just could not hack it on your own."

"Okay already, don't rub it in. Yes, he and I were best friends. He did a lot for me, but I did a lot for him, too. Except for Caroline, nobody was closer to him;

the three of us did everything together. Two jocks and a nerd, that's what you guys called us. He even asked his mom if I could come along that time when they went to Hilton Island for Christmas vacation. But look what he's doing now. I can't understand it." As he spoke, he opened his notebook computer and looked up the *New York Post* story that had made him so mad. Jose moved over to get a better view of the screen.

When he saw the picture in the middle of the article about the rapid growth of Jason Housten's company, he exclaimed, "Man, look at that babe on Jason's arm! She's something else! Is he dating that beauty?"

"Nah, he claims he has to be seen with beautiful women in order to promote his image, which helps him promote his company. I don't know if I believe him or not, but in the meantime he is hurting the hell out of Caroline. That makes me pretty damn mad."

"So what are you so upset about? Are you jealous that he is going around with a lot of beautiful women? Or the success of his company?"

"I'm just pissed off at the way all this hurts Caroline."

"I don't know if she's all that concerned. I saw her last week at Wendy Messing's party and she was raving about how well Jason was doing. She showed me a *Wall Street Journal* article about Milbank, his company. She was gloating over the news that the stock had more than tripled in the last half-year." Jose paused and looked at Reggie, a smile forming around his lips. "You like her a lot don't you? When we were still in school and I saw the three of you together, I suspected you had the hots for her but did not want to compete with Jason."

"Yes, I liked her a lot, but not in that way. The three of us were close. We were pals; but the two of them had a special bond. I was not part of that. She was his gal and that was it. I never thought about her in any other way."

"What the hell happened for you to rag on him now?"

"It did not happen all at once. It took a long time for me to realize what he was all about."

"I certainly never noticed any friction between the two of you. Actually, I was amazed how freely he would lend you that fancy sports car of his."

"Yes, he did. He was amazingly generous in that way. Whenever my old jalopy let me down, he would just hand me the keys. Not only that, he never made a big deal about things he could afford and I couldn't. He would just make sure I could, and never claimed any credit for it. Nobody needed to know."

"So when did things go wrong?"

"Our first real argument was when he told me that he told Caroline he wouldn't be going to Syracuse with her. The two of them had been talking about it for a long time, and she was thrilled when they both were accepted. Her excitement rubbed off on me. I was even a little jealous that I would not be joining them. Jason and I had a huge argument about it. I told him he was stupid, Syracuse was a great school, and he had no right doing that to Caroline."

"The two of you stopped talking? Was that what broke up your friendship?"

"No, I let it go, but it was the first time I saw this selfish streak in him. This attitude of his continued when they went to college. He did not seem to care much that Caroline decided not to go to Syracuse by herself. I know she was devastated; she never imagined they wouldn't go together and that she would be separated from him. She stayed close to home and went to Suffix Community College and continued to live with Jason's mother. She never showed her disappointment. On the contrary, she always talked about how proud she was of Jason. But he didn't show much concern for her. While he was at MIT he almost never invited her to come visit. But even though the guy makes me angry, I must admit the man is a genius."

"What makes you say that?"

"That company of his, Milbank, it's unbelievable what he has made of it in a very short time. During his second semester at MIT he went to a seminar in which one of his professors discussed the pending liquidation of Milbank, a company owned by Jason's father. The professor explained how the company had invested all their research in the relatively new field of neuro-electronics and failed to explore other possible applications for their new technology.

"When Jason quit MIT after his freshman year, his father asked him to join his company. As I heard it, the offer was very lucrative, but Jason turned it down. He told his dad he had no interest in the commodities branch. He wanted to go into electronics, and he had some ideas he wanted to pursue. His dad was disappointed but agreed. He asked Jason how much he thought he needed to get started. As you know, his dad sits on billions. Jason surprised his dad. He asked for Milbank, a failed company his dad was about to liquidate."

"Milbank was failing when Jason got control?"

"Yes. If his dad wasn't so socially minded it should have gone bankrupt. Instead he was slowly liquidating the company so no one would get hurt. Milbank was his only venture into electronics. It was an outlier in his many industrial holdings. He had invested in Milbank to help the company further develop a very promising apparatus to help paralyzed people gain some control over their limbs. The project never lived up to expectations. After years of research and many prototypes, it was finally decided to call it quits.

"You can imagine his dad's reaction when all Jason asked for was this failing company. At first his dad turned him down, but Jason was persuasive. He told his dad about his plan to use the proprietary electronics developed for the failed project for entirely different purposes.

"Mr. Housten believed in his son and gave him the company, plus several million dollars to help him get started on a totally different project.

"As I said, Jason is a genius. In a few years Milbank, using the proprietary chips and electronic systems originally developed for the failed project, started producing extremely fast computers. Despite being as fast as or faster than anything else on the market, Milbank computers are easy to program and can be used for vastly different tasks. The weapons industry started using them in some of the most sophisticated artillery and in the latest jet fighters. Even NASA has incorporated them in their latest projects.

"The only downside for Milbank is that the most advanced version of their computer, the UT 500, unlike all the other versions, can't be exported or sold to a foreign entity. So they have to watch that carefully. If the company violates this ban on exporting that high-end version, Jason, as the CEO, could be facing a long time in jail."

"Sounds like you have been following Jason's career pretty closely. Reggie, are you sure you're not a tad bit jealous of your old pal's success?"

"I can honestly say no. I can't live like that. In high school Jason, Caroline, and I were the center of a group of close friends. You were part of it and it was comfortable knowing who our friends were, who we could rely on. As they say, 'who would have your back,' regardless. You and I still have most of that group around us. I have no ambition to be anyone but Reggie McLaughlin, manager of old man Samson's hardware store on Main Street. I know who I am and I wouldn't change that for the lonely life Jason must be living. Does he have any true friends? I think not. How can he possibly know the difference between friends and people who hang around him based on his success and, of course, his wealth? I know of only one true friend who is totally devoted to him."

"Of course you mean Caroline. You sound like Jason's personal historian. What else do you know about him?"

"Milbank, Jason's factory, is located in Syosset, New York, just over thirty miles from New York City. When he took over the factory, Jason moved to Syosset. He bought a cute little house near the factory complex but was seldom there. He spent almost all his time in the factory supervising research, much of which he did himself. His office in the factory had a bathroom and a small sitting room right across the hall. Jason had a bed brought into the sitting room and that is where he lived. For all intents and purposes that was his home."

"He never asked Caroline to move to Syosset and come live with him in that cottage?"

"Are you kidding? He was obsessed with his research and did not have time for anything else. Certainly not for Caroline."

"Uh-oh. Do I hear a touch of anger? Are you sure you don't have some special feelings for that girl? Maybe you are in love with her."

"Stop it already! I told you she is a good friend but no more. I'm not in love with her! Do you want me to continue telling you about Jason or not?"

"Yeah, continue. This is interesting. I never heard much about him after we graduated."

"One of the first things Jason did after he got control of Milbank was to rehire Jeffrey Milkowsky.

A year earlier, Jeffrey had been fired for repeatedly spending time researching things that had little to do with the project at hand. Jeffrey was known for this. He would get some idea in his head and he would try to develop it at the expense of the research he was hired to do. Jeffrey was a brilliant electronics engineer, but word had gotten around and no one would hire him. Jason had heard about the things Jeffrey was working on while at Milbank. This was exactly what his professor at MIT had touched on and what Jason was now working on. Together Jason and Jeffrey started working on a whole new system of supercomputing. They reached a breakthrough almost immediately, and within a year they were able to show the first prototype. Their success after that has been phenomenal."

Jose Alvares shook his head in amazement. "That nerd Jason. He might become even richer than his father. Maybe I should have kept closer contact with him. Like you said, he was always quite generous; who knows what he might have given me?"

"Shut up. I know you don't mean that."

"Calm down, Reggie. I was only kidding! But you are right; the way he seems to have treated Caroline is less than I expected from him."

V

After the first generation of Milbank computers hit the market, Alpine Crest, a leading electronics manufacturer, brought out a competing model. Jason sprang into action and developed plans to take over his much larger competitor. His dad was not willing to help him finance a hostile takeover bid. So Jason enlisted the help of Jerry Collins, the head of a venture capital firm on the West Coast. Jason knew that Jerry was not averse to helping dislodge the management of companies that were cash heavy and vulnerable to takeover. What seemed like an easy takeover turned into a long, drawn-out, messy affair. In the end, Jason and Jerry prevailed, and Jason immediately proceeded to merge Milbank into the much larger Alpine Crest. Due to its rapid growth, the capitalization of Milbank was large enough to give Jason control. He became the CEO. Jerry had to settle for the COO position. The two of them made a formidable duo. They renamed the company

Milbank Industries and proceeded to take over the top end of the supercomputer market.

Jason's emphasis switched from research to sales. Milbank Industries was in a position to hire top scientists and engineers for their research and development. Jason discovered that it was much more exciting to travel all over the world than to spend all his time in research. To be in a position to better manage Milbank Industries, he decided to move to New York City. He bought a deluxe apartment on Central Park West. While the apartment was being painted, and one of the rooms was being prepared to be his office, Jason went to see his two biggest fans, his mother and Caroline. The two of them religiously followed every step of his success and when they saw pictures of his new apartment they felt they had shared in his success.

On the morning Jason was scheduled to leave for New York City, Caroline said, "It's such a beautiful day, let's go for a ride. I want to show you the new extension they built on our old high school. You won't believe how big the place has gotten."

Instead of heading for the high school, Caroline drove to the Holly Day Inn a few miles out of town.

Jason was confused and asked, "What are you doing? This isn't anywhere near the high school."

"Don't ask. Just play along. I have reserved a room for us, and I have a big surprise for you."

Jason was uncomfortable when Caroline checked them in as Mr. and Mrs. Smith. The credit card she handed the desk clerk obviously did not match the name but the clerk said nothing.

When they got to their room Jason said, "I thought we agreed—"

Caroline quickly hushed him up and pushed him into the room. She had barely closed the door behind her when she started stripping her clothes off. Totally nude, she turned to face Jason. He stared at her nude body. It was not as if he had never seen her naked before. During the time they had been going steady they had often made out in the nude. But each time he had been the instigator and she was always more discreet about being totally naked. They had always held back and never gone all the way before. As a bewildered Jason continued to stare at her, Caroline aggressively pulled his clothes off.

She stepped back and cupped her breasts. "While you're in New York City, I want you to have more than these two to remember me by." As she pushed him onto the bed she said, "I want you; I have always wanted to feel you in me. I want that before you leave for New York City."

For both of them it was not quite what they had expected. Neither of them dared mention it. They did not say much when they got dressed and awkwardly sat around the motel room.

Finally, Caroline said, "Let's go home. It's getting late; Mom will be wondering what's keeping us."

VI

Several months later, while Jason was on a conference call, the doorman buzzed him. "There is a gentleman here to see you. Can I send him up?"

Jason was not expecting anybody. "Who is it?" he asked.

"It's Mr. Housten, your father."

"Send him up." Jason excused himself and hung up the phone. *What in the hell is my dad doing here? Haven't seen or heard from him in months. I thought he was still fuming about that hostile takeover and that we ditched the former management.*

There was an authoritative knock on the door and Jason opened it. He greeted his dad with, "I didn't expect to see you here. I thought you were mad at me."

"Mad is too strong. I'm disappointed in the way you went after Alpine Crest. You could have just negotiated a merger. I would have helped finance any deal they proposed."

"Wouldn't have worked. I went to talk to them. I met with their full board of directors. They practically kicked me out the door. They treated me like some kid who wanted to play in the big leagues. They told me a company like theirs, long an icon in the industry, would never negotiate with an upstart like Milbank."

"Why didn't you tell me about that?"

"Come on, get serious. Tell you about it? I tried but you were always too involved in your own business to take the time to hear me out. All you really paid attention to was that I asked for help in financing a proxy battle. I still hurt from the scolding you gave me for getting involved in a hostile takeover."

"I'm sorry, son. I didn't know all the facts."

"Where have I heard that before? But okay, to what do I owe this honor?"

"Your mother called me and asked that I come and talk to you about Caroline."

"What about Caroline, and how did you get involved? Why didn't she just call me?"

"You would have to ask her that. Maybe she thinks you wouldn't listen to her. I guess she has spoken to you many times before about this."

"What is this?"

"Your relationship with Caroline and how you treat her. The girl is beyond crazy about you. She supports you in everything you do and basks in all your achievements. She is really very proud of you, and that's why she is afraid to do anything that might hinder you from reaching your goals. Your mom and I think you take unfair advantage of this. We think you do love her, but it is always all about you. You do what you want without any consideration of what she might want."

"Excuse me! You should talk. Leaving Mom for some damn floozy was okay? It was all right for you to betray her? That wasn't selfish? Who are you to come here and lecture me?" Jason got red in the face as he spat out the words. His father paused before he responded. In a way he had expected this and he was hoping this was the time he could explain to his son what happened years ago to drive him and his mother apart.

"I know I deserved that. I have always wanted to explain things to you, but it felt so awkward to talk about it. It's hard for a father to discuss the details with his son about his relationship with his wife, especially when it comes to sex. Besides, you were never really open to hearing my side of the story, and in a way, I was proud of the way you stood up for her. In your eyes she was right, end of story. You never wavered. Maybe the time has come that we start listening to each other."

Jason never expected this turn in the conversation. His father had always been this tall, imposing figure, both physically and emotionally, difficult to reach out to.

"Maybe I said too much. Sit down and I'll pour you a drink. Scotch okay?"

"Scotch would be fine."

When they both were seated in the huge leather chairs in front of the picture window overlooking

Central Park, Jason said, "Okay, I'm listening, but I don't want to hear one bad word about my mother."

Jason's father took a long swig. "Scotch helps, but it is still hard to talk about. I have always felt that I got caught in a perfect storm, but I know that won't excuse in your eyes what happened."

After a long pause, he continued. "It all started when an oil storage tank exploded in our depot in the Harbor of Rotterdam. There was a chain reaction and before they could contain the fire, most of our depot was burning. I was in our office in Germany, but saw the whole thing on television. Flames shot thousands of feet into the sky and the explosions could be heard halfway to Amsterdam. There were many casualties, not only among our own personnel but also among the firefighters who tried to contain the fire. The investigation as to the cause of the explosion revealed several instances of negligence on our part, the worst being a serious flaw in the construction of the tank that caused the initial explosion. The European press was quick to blame it on Yankee greed. They claimed we purposely cut corners in order to save money. The depot was run by Tom Frederick. Tom had been working for us for over twenty years. He was very capable, and I trusted him completely. I had to admit I never checked on the operation of that depot, and I never suspected that they approved cheaper building materials in order to save on the construction of new storage tanks. Besides being a long-time employee, Tom was a dear friend. I was heartbroken when he and two other managers were sentenced to long-term jail sentences for knowingly allowing the inferior tanks to be built. For months I walked around in a state of depression. It did not help that I received tons of mail calling me a murderer, blaming me for what happened. As the company CEO I was ultimately responsible, and I should have checked more carefully as to what was happening in the organization.

"At that time Mildred, my long-time personal assistant, retired, and Jennifer Douglas replaced her. Jennifer was not a classic beauty like your mother, but she was very cute and really sexy. I don't know who in HR hired her, but I expect they hoped her bubbly personality would help cheer me up. Her personnel file told me she was forty, but she looked like she was in her early twenties and she dressed the part. Not that she ever looked cheap, but she knew how to dress so her clothes would show off the best parts of her youthful figure.

"Jennifer and I hit it off from the start. She did her best to cheer me up whenever another barrage of hate mail arrived from Europe. Eventually, she made sure she arrived at the office early enough to go through my mail and throw out the worst of the hate mail before I arrived. To protect me further, she arranged a new personal e-mail address for me, which she only gave out on a need-to-know basis. She cancelled my old e-mail address. Actually, that was against my long-standing policy of being an easily accessible CEO. But I went along with all those measures to isolate me. It felt comfortable to be shielded from all the bad stuff, and without those distractions I could fully concentrate on rebuilding the image of our company."

"Of course I heard about the explosion, but I had no idea the consequences were that serious and how that affected you."

"Nothing bad about your mother. I loved her dearly, but she did not like problems. She had this habit of blotting them out; we never discussed the after effects of the explosion at home."

"You mean to tell me you two never discussed the explosion?"

"No, it wasn't that extreme. We did discuss what happened and the international coverage it received. But we never went into the outrage against me personally and my heartache of seeing my friend, Tom Frederick, sentenced to spend twenty years in jail, which probably meant for the rest of his life."

"You kept all of that from me. I had no idea the situation was that serious."

"I don't think it was the type of thing you discuss with a thirteen-year-old. And certainly not when his mother always shielded him from bad news. Anyway, don't get me sidetracked; I'm trying to explain why your mother and I split up.

"The court in the Netherlands turned down the amount we offered to compensate the injured and the families of those who lost their lives. We had already paid huge sums to compensate the city of Rotterdam for the damage. I was worried about the financial stability of my company. Could we survive this? I had been in conference for most of the day with our lawyers and accountants to discuss what our total exposure would amount to. The situation did not look good. It was past nine that evening and I was still going over the figures they gave me when Jennifer stepped back into my office.

"'What in the world are you still doing here?' I asked.

"'I could ask you the same,' she replied. 'Sitting at that desk feeling sorry for yourself isn't going to solve anything. Besides, I know you'll get through this. The Noah Housten I know doesn't let a problem like this knock him down. He'll rebuild, I know he will. Come on, get your coat; I'll buy you a drink.'

"At that time, our main office was still here in New York City, on Park Avenue South. We lived in Connecticut in the same house as when you were born. I was tempted, but did not feel it was right to go out for drinks with Jennifer at that late hour.

"Jennifer persisted. 'Come on, don't be like that. A drink will do you good. It will take your mind off all those dreary discussions you had all day. Let's just hop over to the Park Bar on East Fifteenth Street.'

"I told her I never heard of it

"She laughed. 'Well, it's not as fancy as the Top of the Sixes or any of the other places you usually go to. It's an intimate tin-ceilinged cocktail spot just off Union Square. That's where the post-work crowd goes. You'll love it.'

"I said we would have to take a taxi; I let Alfredo, my driver, go, and was planning to take a limo home.

"'No problem', she said. 'I'll call for one now.'

"When we got to the Park Bar the place was packed, but Jenifer knew most of the staff and we got a table right away. Besides the staff, Jenifer knew a lot of other people, and we switched tables to join a group of her friends. It was a great group of interesting people and I got into some animated conversations. Before we knew it, it was three o'clock, the place was practically empty, and it was time to go home. We managed to get a cab. The plan was to bring Jennifer home first, and from there I would call the limo service to take me home to Connecticut. When I called the limo service they informed me they had already let all the drivers go for the night and would have none available till they reported for their six o'clock shift. I told Jennifer I would try to get another cab to take me to a nearby hotel or even back to the office.

"She protested, 'That's crazy, just stay here. It's too late to go anyplace now.' We argued about it for a while and I finally gave in. Before going to sleep we sat down for a nightcap. I was sure we would be sleeping in separate bedrooms. I was sitting on the couch in front of the fireplace and Jenifer plopped down very close to me. As we talked she started snuggling up to me and I did not mind that one bit.

"Again, without saying anything bad about your mother, I have to explain that she was not a very physical person. Our mothers introduced us, and from the moment I saw her, I knew I wanted to marry her. Her beauty captivated me, and I'm sure she was attracted to me, too. But we rarely made love.

There is a reason you are an only child. I'm sorry to say your mother is somewhat frigid."

Jason was not surprised, nor was he embarrassed by his dad using that expression. He told his dad, "To me that showed her character. It made my life a lot easier. After the divorce she never had any boyfriends. She never even went out on a date. Not that men did not try to ask her out. As you said, Mom is a beautiful woman."

Jason's dad continued, "Jennifer coming on to me was exciting; it felt great, and no way was I going to stop her. We started kissing and she placed my hands on her most exciting parts. You're my son and I will not explain any further. Enough said. I slept with her that night.

"That would have been a onetime indiscretion but for the fact that one of the secretaries from my company had seen us at the Park Bar. I had told your mother that the meetings ran late and I had decided to stay in town that night. But she had received an anonymous call from someone telling her she had seen Jennifer and me in a cozy little bar late that night. When your mother confronted me with it, I admitted that the two of us had been out till very late that night. When she asked if anything had happened between Jennifer and me, I admitted to having slept with her. I was promptly relegated to a guest bedroom and from then on our conversation was reduced to yes and no."

Jason looked at his dad. The man had never looked so human and vulnerable to him. His broad shoulders were hunched over and the usual confident look was gone from his handsome face. "Couldn't you just admit to having gone out for drinks after a really shitty day? Did you have to tell her you slept with that woman?"

"I respected your mother too much to lie to her. Our relationship was by no means perfect, but it was honest. I thought that in time we could patch things up. I had Jennifer transferred to another department and recommended she be promoted and given a responsible position at one of our branch offices overseas. That did not work out. Your mother would not forgive me. She couldn't understand that I was close to a deep depression and that I would respond to this sexual encounter. After a while, I stopped being so hard on myself about cheating on your mother. I realized I had been longing for a hot sexual affair; I started blaming your mother for not giving in to more than some impersonal encounters when I wanted to make love to her. I convinced myself she helped drive me into the arms of Jennifer.

"I carefully avoided any contact with Jenifer. Since the department she was now working in was fifteen floors down from my office, I was pretty sure I would not accidently bump into her.

"But she managed to storm unannounced into my office. 'Thanks for having me transferred to Australia. You could have asked; I don't want to go to fucking Australia. Don't worry, I resigned today. You won't have to worry about having me around. Look, I apologize for what happened. Maybe I should not have led you on, but I'm not sorry I slept with you. For me it wasn't just sex; we made love. At least I did. If you did not notice, I fell in love with you. I know, don't fall in love with your boss; it will only get you into trouble. Okay, it did. If the feeling was mutual, come to my apartment tonight, I'll be waiting for you. If you don't show up, I'll know I was delusional about the famous Noah Housten being in love with me and I'll disappear out of your life. Please don't insult me by offering me money.'

"I went to her apartment that evening and after your mother and I got a divorce, I married her. We had a great few years together. I bought a huge estate in Kings Point on Long Island and we had bushels of friends come out on weekends. Some stayed the night. A frequent visitor was Arnold Thomson, the slugging outfielder for the New York Yankees. He was staying at the house when I was in Japan negotiating a large oil contract.

"When I returned from that trip, Royston, the butler, approached me with the following message. 'I'll probably be fired for telling you this, but you are my employer and you have always treated me awfully well.'

"I was anxious to hear what the man had to say and I urged him to speak up. He looked away when he said, 'I could not help but notice that Mr. Thomson did not spend the last several nights in the guest room assigned to him. I am obliged to tell you he spent the nights with Miss Jennifer in your room.' Royston did not get fired, but I did divorce Jennifer.

"Now that I have bared myself in front of you, will you listen to a man who has learned some lessons the hard way? I have come to tell you that Caroline is planning to come to see you. She'll be here this coming Friday, and your mother and I want you to stop putting her on hold until **you** are ready to get married. Enough of what **you** want. It's time to do what Caroline wants. She has been patient and indulged you way too long. You've been stringing her along for about six years now. That's way too long! We know the two of you are in love. You wouldn't still be going together after all these years if you weren't. Don't be a fool. Don't let a girl who is so deeply in love with you go. If you stall much longer she might slip through your fingers, and you'll regret it for the rest of your life. Go ahead, marry her. You already have this gorgeous apartment for the two of you to live in. Or move to Connecticut, buy a big house. You can afford it."

Jason let his father finish before responding. His father expected to hear all sorts of protests but Jason was very reasonable.

"You gave me a lot to think about. About Caroline, for sure, but also about you and Mom. I have to reevaluate how I feel about your break-up and how that has influenced my relationship with Caroline."

VII

Punctually as ever, Caroline arrived exactly at seven on Friday evening. When Jason opened the door she flew into his arms. "Boy, have I missed you! It's been more than a month since you came to see us." She hugged him and kissed him again and again. "Hey, how about kissing me back? Don't just stand there; I want a big, long, juicy kiss. Show me how much you missed me."

Jason laughed it off and responded with a slight hug. "Come on in; we can't stand in the hall forever." He grabbed her suitcase and carried it in. "I'll bring it directly to your room."

"My room? What's that all about? Why can't I stay with you in your room? I thought we settled that the day you left for New York."

"We still have to keep up appearances. What if Mom asks? I bet she still thinks you are a virgin."

Caroline was not at all pleased by this welcome. "I somehow doubt that she is unaware. She knows we are human. But if you insist, I'll send her a picture of me sleeping in your guest room."

After that somewhat rocky start, things settled down and the two of them sat down to catch up on the latest news on both fronts. Caroline had lots of news about things that were happening back home, and Jason enjoyed hearing all the latest gossip about their friends. Who was sleeping with who was always big news, especially if it was about people you would never think of being attracted to each other, like Reggie McLaughlin and Wendy Messing.

When Jason finished telling Caroline about the new contracts he had secured for Milbank Industries he said, "Come on, get dressed; I hope you brought something formal to wear. We are going to someplace really special for dinner."

"Really?" Caroline's face lit up and forgotten was the disappointment on arrival. "Great, I have just the thing to wear. Tell me, where are we going?"

"Have you ever heard of Tahaka Miyazuki, the famous Japanese film producer?"

"Of course I have. He produced *Princess of the Moving Castle* and many other well-known animated movies."

"Well, he has invited us to join him tonight for dinner at Masa, his favorite sushi restaurant."

Caroline could hardly contain her excitement. "How in the world did you ever meet Tahaka Miyazuki?"

"A family member of his is involved in a Japanese government program to build a fleet of coastal patrol boats. While I was in Japan to negotiate the purchase of several hundred of our CP 1500 computers for those boats, I met with his nephew. The guy is an electronics nut like me and we struck it off right away. He invited me to his house, and there I met his uncle, Tahaka Miyazuki. Yesterday, Tahaka himself called me. He and his nephew are in town on a private vacation and he wanted to know if I could join the two of them today for dinner at Masa. Masa is absolutely the most expensive restaurant in town. I told him I would love to, but you were coming to New York to see me.

"'Bring her, of course,' was his spontaneous reply, and so you and I are going to dinner with none other than Tahaka Miyazuki. I hope you like sushi."

"I love it. Don't you remember my stepfather used to take us to the sushi restaurant on Main Street? You probably don't remember. That was long before the incident. Before I moved in with your mom and you."

VIII

"That was fantastic. No, fantastic is much too mild to describe a dinner like that. The whole evening was beyond! What an interesting man. I could listen all night to Mr. Tahaka telling stories about his youth in Japan." Caroline was floating on a cloud and during the entire taxi ride home she could not stop talking about their evening with Tahaka Miyazuki. Once inside the apartment, she jumped all over Jason to thank him for taking her.

The dinner had taken a long time from start to finish and it was time to go to bed. Caroline disappeared into the guest room. She game out wearing her brand-new Angel Sleep Tee pajamas and headed for Jason's bedroom. She stopped in her tracks when Jason said, "We shouldn't do that. The time in the motel was great but we should hold back. We're not married, and we agreed to wait. In the past when we made out and you were worried that I would try to go too far, I always told you I respected you too much to attempt to go all the way before we were married. I have thought about it, and I think what we did in the motel was a little premature."

Caroline could not believe what she was hearing. "I wanted it. I thought we both wanted it. I shared my body with you and I felt you inside me. And you say that was a mistake? My God, what has come over you? Are you saying we only fucked and we did not make love?"

"Of course not! I did not mean that at all. All I'm saying is we always planned to wait until we were married, and we should not start sleeping together regularly just because we did it one time."

Caroline turned and ran back into the guest room and threw herself on the bed. Jason could hear her violent sobbing even though she had slammed the door shut.

He opened the door and approached the bed. "Caroline, please stop crying. It's something we always agreed upon. Why are you getting so upset over it now?"

Caroline sat up and faced him. "Get out of the room! Please leave, I have to be alone right now."

Jason protested, "I said nothing we hadn't previously agreed on."

"Get out! Please get out and leave me alone. If you don't understand how I feel, I can't explain it to you. And I won't even try. Just get out."

Jason went back to his room and got ready for bed. He tried to go to sleep, but Caroline's continued sobbing kept him awake. At times it was so bad it sounded like she was being operated on without painkillers.

Finally, Jason could not stand it any longer; he went back into the guest room. "Caroline, please calm down. Nothing has changed; we are back to where we have always been. Yes, we strayed once, but that does not mean we have to continue."

With her eyes swollen almost shut from crying, Caroline sat up in the bed. "Maybe for you nothing has changed, but my world has been turned upside down." She held up her hand, signaling for Jason not to respond; she wasn't finished talking. "We did not 'just stray' in that hotel room. Over the years you were my everything. My hero, my love. Damn it. You were my god. I loved you so much, I lost sight of everything else. I refused to accept that you were stalling all along; that you really did not intend to marry me. Yes, I instigated what we did in that hotel room. I loved you so much, I couldn't wait any longer. I was no longer satisfied with our extended petting; I needed to make real love to you. The horrible truth is, despite the fact that you reject me, I still love you. I must be sick or something. I now know you don't want me, but I still want you."

"Sweetheart, it's not that I don't want you. Please accept that I really loved you for all these years. In many ways I still love you, but I know it just won't work. I'm addicted to the type of life I lead. The emotional rush of bringing new products to market. Products others tried to make but failed. The excitement of traveling all over the world and meeting famous and influential people. I can't give it up for married life. I would make your life miserable."

"What makes you think I couldn't live with that? I have never tried to stop you from doing all those things. On the contrary, I have always been your biggest cheerleader."

"Yes, you have. And you must know, I have a selfish streak I can't control. I know I have hurt you many times by totally ignoring your wishes and doing only what I wanted. This might sound disingenuous, but I love you too much to keep hurting you. But I can't stop myself. I can't change. And it's better for us to face the truth now rather than after we get involved in a failed marriage like that of my parents."

Caroline seemed to have calmed down but her big, brown eyes were bloodshot and her normally perfect hairdo was all messed up, hiding much of her pretty face. Looking at her crouched into a ball on the bed, one heap of misery, Jason could see that she was devastated.

"I just wish you could have been my real brother rather than the pretend brother I was in love with. I think love between siblings is a hell of a lot easier than this. Boy, this hurts. I love you so much I could scream, 'Don't push me away!' At the same time I love you enough not to ask you to do something you can't. I never dreamed I would one day have to give you up, but I won't tie you down. Good night, Jason. Leave me alone now. I'll be gone early in the morning."

IX

"**C**ome on, Kristy. Hurry up and get dressed! Hawkins, my driver, will be here in less than twenty minutes to take me to the airport." Jason was already fully dressed. He went into the bedroom to see what was keeping Kristy. As he entered his bedroom, Kristy was coming out of the bathroom still wearing nothing but the sheer bikini panties she had slept in.

"Why can't I just stay here while you are gone?"

"Not again! We've been over this time and time again. When I am out of town you stay in your own apartment; not here."

"But why? I see no good reason for it. It's not like I will steal anything."

"I don't feel like going over this again. You can't stay here while I'm gone. That's the way I want it. Besides, you have a nice apartment of your own. You'd better like it; I pay enough rent for the place."

Kristy Holoway stretched her arms above her head, as if she was trying to wake up. Jason knew darn well what she was doing. She was giving him a good look at her beautiful body in an attempt to entice him into changing his mind.

Her gesture made Jason smile. "That works better when I have time to enjoy what you are offering but I'm in a hurry. I have to catch my plane to Hong Kong." He did take a moment to enjoy the view. Her long legs seamlessly flowed into her panties, highlighting her perfect body. "Turn around; you might as well show me the whole package." Kristy gracefully turned to show the rest. She was a tall girl and Jason thought to himself, *I can't decide if that provocatively sticking out behind of hers is one of her better features or a blemish on her otherwise perfect figure. What she got physically she never got in brains.* Jason wasn't complaining about that. He preferred gorgeous girls that were dumb. That made it easy not to get emotionally involved with them.

"Show is over, kid. You really have to hurry and get dressed. I'll tell the doorman to get you a cab when you get ready to leave. I have to go now. See you in ten days."

"Hold on, not so fast. You have to kiss me good-bye. Remember to leave those Asian beauties alone. I don't like competing." She made sure he could feel her naked body as she bent down to kiss him. At six foot one she was almost three inches taller than Jason.

The black Mercedes S was waiting for him in front of the building. Before Hawkins could get out to open the door, the doorman had already reached the car. He knew Jason never sat in back, and he opened the passenger-side door for him.

"Going to be gone for a while, Mr. Housten?"

"Should be back in ten days. Martin, could you please get a cab for Miss Holoway when she comes down?"

"Of course, Mr. Housten. I'll take care of it. She does not have to worry about that. Anything else you want me to take care of while you are gone?"

"Nothing special, thank you, Martin. Take care, see you in ten days."

Hawkins was in a chatty mood, and on the way to the airport Jason heard all about Hawkins' eldest son being selected for his little league travel team. Jason spontaneously volunteered to sponsor the team.

When Hawkins dropped him off in front of the departure hall, Jason reminded him, "Don't forget to remind me, when I get back, what you'll need by way of a budget. I want them to have nice uniforms. The kids can decide what name they want for their team. If the league does not provide all the equipment, go ahead and order some good stuff."

"That's very generous of you, Mr. Housten. The kids will be excited to have a sponsor!"

Jason waved it off and disappeared into the departure hall.

X

"**W**ould you like another drink, sir?" Jason looked up from the thick binder lying on the table in front of him. The flight attendant was holding a tray with several different drinks on it.

"A Coke would be nice, thank you," Jason replied as he moved the binder to make room on the tray. Just as the flight attendant reached over to place the glass of Coke on Jason's tray, a man burst into the first-class compartment.

He was wielding what looked like a cell phone and he yelled, "If I push the send button this whole damned plane will explode! Do exactly what I say or I'll do it." The flight attendant spilled the entire glass of Coke over Jason's binder. She turned to face the man but he pushed her aside and headed for the cockpit door. Moments later a second man came into the first-class cabin. Wielding a box cutter, he roughly pushed the purser in front of him. The first intruder grabbed the flight attendant and demanded that she open the cockpit door.

She was shaking like a leaf and mumbled, "I can't. It's locked from the inside."

"Then tell the pilots to open it."

The purser stepped in front of the flight attendant. "No way will they open that door for scum like you."

"Open the door! Tell them to open the fucking door! Tell them! I'll cut your fucking head off if they don't!" The second intruder added a physical threat to his words and pushed his box cutter blade against the throat of the purser.

All this was happening in the aisle right next to Jason's seat. The man wielding the box cutter heard Jason say to the purser, "Inform the pilots we have terrorists aboard and under no circumstances should they open the door."

"So we have a hero. I'll show you who is hero." With that he dragged Jason out of his seat and threw him to the floor. Next he proceeded to kick him; Jason pulled up his legs trying to protect his private parts. A third terrorist came in from the business-class cabin.

"Danat! Stop that. We have to get to Germany to release our brothers; Shalkar, Temir, and Yeleu, and I don't need any of your temper tantrums to mess up our plans. Pick the man up and bring him over to me." Jason was roughly hoisted up by his armpits and deposited in front of Wali.

Wali, obviously the leader of the hijackers, didn't look at all like a terrorist. He had on a nice grey suit and looked more like a clean-cut Ivy League student than a man who was in the process of hijacking a plane.

He poured a glass of water and handed it to Jason. "Sorry about that. Danat gets a little rough at times. But your advice to the pilots was wrong, very wrong. Get on the intercom and tell them we packed a massive amount of explosives in our suit-cases. Brand-new stuff that cannot be detected by the scanners at the airport. Each of our cell phones is programmed to send a signal that will set off the entire amount. That would blow this plane right out of the air. Do we want to do that? Of course not. But we will if all of you don't cooperate with us."

Jason looked closely at Wali, trying to size him up. Who was this nice-looking young man? What did he want? He did not have to wait long to find out.

"We are part of Cras Es Noster (Tomorrow Is ours). Our group is dedicated to taking back what you in the West have stolen from us. For years the West has stolen our natural resources. You even robbed us of the fruits of our labor. The time has come for the people of the East to take back what is rightfully ours."

Jason had heard about Cras Es Noster. For three years the group had terrorized financial cen-ters around the world. Their latest raid had been in Frankfurt, Germany. In a vain attempt to steal the gold reserves of Germany, twelve members of Cras Es Noster stormed the Deutsche Bundesbank. In the shootout with the German police that ensued, forty-seven people were killed. Among them were two police officers and nine members of Cras Es Noster. Three of the attackers were captured and were being held under maximum security in a Frankfurt jail.

Wali continued, "We intend to gain the release of our brothers who are held in Frankfurt. If the Germans reject our demands, we'll blow up this plane with everybody in it. If that kills us too, so be it. The world has to learn that we are a force to be reckoned with, and a few more casualties among our ranks won't be enough to stop us"

Jason tried to keep his voice under control and sound convincing when he said, "You'll never get away with it. We all heard about the raid in Frankfurt and the way your group slaughtered all those people. The Germans will never release those murderers."

"You'll be surprised. By the way, my brothers are not murderers. They fought for a rightful cause. It's the German police and their brutal tactics that caused those casualties. And now, whether you like it or not, you are going to help me. While my colleagues and I control the passengers, you are going to persuade the pilots to head for Frankfurt. Once this plane has turned around, I'll come in and negotiate with the Germans."

"No way! I won't cooperate with you."

"Oh yes you will!" Wali went over to the intercom and barked into it, "Open the door! A passenger is coming in with a message. If you don't comply in the next three minutes I'll start executing passengers every two minutes until you open the door!" To show he meant it he pulled out a pistol, which he aimed at Jason's head."

The pistol surprised Jason. "How did you manage to get that aboard?"

"You in the West aren't as smart as you think you are." The cynical smile on his face transformed his boyish face into a cruel mask. The friendly baby blue eyes were gone and he stared with an ice-cold glare at Jason. "You make three dimensional printers freely available and then you are surprised that people make their own plastic pistols." Once more he barked into the intercom. "The countdown has started. Are you ready to open up? My pistol is pointed at the head of the first victim!"

To Jason's relief, the door swung open. Wali pushed him in with such great force that he tumbled past the pilots and landed against the instrument panel.

The pilot helped him up and said, "What in the hell is going on out there? Was it wrong to open the door? Would he have started killing?"

Jason wiped the blood off his lip, which had split open when he landed against the side stick controllers before he hit the main instrument panel. "Yes! He is deadly serious. They are part the Cras Es Noster movement who perpetrated that bloody attack on the bank in Frankfurt last week. They think they can gain the release of the three surviving terrorists by threatening to blow up this plane."

"Are they capable of that?"

"I'm pretty sure they can. Their leader, the one you heard on the intercom, says they have a lot of explosives packed in their suitcases. He says they can set it off using their cell phones. He claims it is some new stuff that cannot be detected by airport scanners. I believe him because he also has this plastic pistol that he claims they made on a 3-D printer."

A voice came over the speaker. "The captain already connected us here at flight control. We heard what you said. Do you know what their demands are?"

"He wants me to persuade the pilots to head for Frankfurt. Once the plane is heading there he will come into the cockpit to negotiate with German authorities about the release of the three terrorists held in Frankfurt."

"This comes from the highest authority here at flight control. 'We will not give permission to divert your plane to Frankfurt. Pilot has final responsibility and can take action based on further developments.' We will continue to monitor."

The pilot looked at his copilot and signaled the standby pilot, who was scheduled to fly the second lap from Tokyo to Hong Kong, to come over and consult with him. "This has always been my worst nightmare." Turning to Jason he asked, "Do you think we can overpower them?"

"I have no idea how many of them are out there. All I saw were the three in first class, but I'm sure there must be more of them in business and economy. Someone must have been restraining the rest of the flight crew and the passengers. Nobody followed those three, and it's impossible no one in the back noticed what was going on."

"If I bank this plane a couple of times and pretend I changed course, do you think we could go out there and find out exactly how many hijackers we are dealing with?"

"It's worth a try," the stand-by pilot said. He turned to Jason. "Go back out and tell that guy we're heading for Frankfurt. When he comes in here, I'll try to leave and join you. The two of us can try to find out how many of these bastards are aboard this plane."

Just when Jason exited the cockpit, the plane banked sharply. He lost his balance and went flying into Wali, who grabbed him by the shoulders.

Jason told him, "Pilot is heading for Frankfurt, you can go in now." He did not expect Wali's response.

"Good. I'll have to check his instruments to make sure."

"You know how to do that?"

"I'm a licensed pilot. I may not be able to fly a big plane, but I know enough to know you don't correct course and start heading to Frankfurt by abruptly making a sharp left turn." Wali grabbed the flight attendant and roughly pushed her in front of him into the cockpit.

"Who the hell do you think you're fooling with that stupid maneuver? Get permission from flight control to change course and have them put you on the fastest route to Frankfurt. Hurry up or I'll blow this young lady's head off!" He grabbed the flight attendant by her hair and pulled her head back. She cried out in pain but her cry was muted when Wali pushed the barrel of his pistol down her throat. The pilot tried to stop him but Wali used his elbow to push him back.

"Any one of you comes any closer and I'll pull the trigger. Now hurry up or you'll get to see the inside of this lady's head."

A calm voice came from the speakers. "This is Major Buchanan in flight control. I cannot see what you are doing to the flight attendant but I order you to stop immediately. I will not negotiate with you about heading for Frankfurt until the pilot tells me you have released the lady."

"The hell you won't. You're not speaking to one of our puppets. You're dealing with Wali Omarov. Don't try to play games with me!"

The major's voice remained calm. "Your English is very good but I detect an accent. Where are you from, Wali? Or do you prefer I address you as Mr. Omarov."

"I really don't care. Just instruct the pilot to change course!"

The major noticed Wali was starting to lose control. "Why are you doing this? We've not done anything to harm you."

"Three brave members of Cras Es Noster are being held in Frankfurt and I am going to free them." Without further warning, Wali pulled the trigger. The back of the flight attendant's head splattered against the cockpit wall. There was blood all over and pieces of brain slowly sliding down the wall onto the floor. The bullet stayed lodged in the wall and did not penetrate the outer skin of the plane. Even though one little bullet hole will not destroy an aircraft, Wali had made sure the muzzle velocity of his plastic pistol would not be enough for the bullet to pass through the aircraft-grade aluminum skin of the fuselage.

He calmly stepped over the lifeless body of the flight attendant and motioned for the pilot to get back in his seat. "Okay, Mr. Major, we are ready to receive the new route that you will clear for us all the way to Rhein-Main International Airport."

The flight crew was in shock. Even though they could not physically see the carnage, the people in the flight control center were just as shocked.

It took a while before Major Buchanan's voice came back over the speaker. "We're working on establishing the route you requested. But before we instruct the pilot with the new route, I must have your assurance that there will be no further casualties. Do I have that?"

"You'll get no such thing from me."

"What good will it do you to get to Frankfurt? The Germans will never give in to your demands."

"We'll see about that. I have six colleagues in the back, ready to blow up this plane on my command. I'm sure the Germans will give in to our demands. If you have any doubts about that, just check the JFK Orange Parking, self-park indoor lot. There you'll find a red Buick in 76B-12. Open the truck and you'll find a suitcase with samples of the explosive material we packed in our suitcases. Tell the Germans what you found. After you inform the Germans we are fully capable of blowing up this plane, they'll give in!"

XI

The plane had been sitting on the tarmac for more than four hours. It was parked on the runway furthest away from the main terminal building. Jason wanted to get away from the terrorists who were constantly walking up and down the aisles keeping an eye out for any sniper who might be approaching the plane. He slid into the vacant window seat next to him. Outside he could see the dozens of police cars and fire engines surrounding the plane. A half-dozen armored personnel carriers had been added to the show of force.

"Get away from that window!" When Jason turned around he looked directly into the glaring face of Danat. As he waved his box cutter at Jason, Danat hissed. "I told Wali you'd be trouble. You've been trying to signal the police."

"They can hardly see me, let alone catch any secret signals."

"I don't care. Next time I catch you looking out the window you'll join the flight attendant in her final

resting place. Now move back into this aisle seat."
Jason knew enough not to argue with Danat and slid
back into his original seat.

Among the terrorists circulating through the
plane was a woman. Each time she passed Jason's
seat she carefully turned her head away and pulled
the heavy scarf covering her face a little tighter.
Despite the fact that she kept her face covered, Jason
thought she looked somewhat familiar. The next
time she passed his seat he leaned into the aisle and
she had to face him to avoid bumping into him. At
that moment, it hit him who it was!

"Ibby?" He tried to keep his voice down so
nobody would hear. She quickly turned away but he
caught her by the arm. "What in the name of God
are you doing here?" he whispered. "Are you an air
marshal?"

The woman pulled loose and fled down the aisle.
Jason got up in order to follow her but another terrorist came flying down the aisle and threw him back
into his seat. "What in the hell do you think you're
doing? Starting a passenger revolt or something?"
He called for Wali to come quickly. "This guy tried to
attack Tanya, he's trouble." Wali recognized Jason as
the messenger he'd sent into the cockpit to persuade
the pilot to change course.

"So now you're turning into a hero? Sorry, I have
no time for heroes."

Jason was scared. He knew what Wali was capable of. "I was just trying to ask her who would be
able to give me permission to go to the bathroom."

"I don't believe you for one moment. Lucky for me I can use you again. I was just about to pick my next example to show the Germans what I'll do if they don't concede to my demands."

Wali grabbed Jason and pulled him to the large exit door. After he got the purser to open it, he pushed Jason in front of him and the two of them stood in the door opening. Wali waited till two men, clad in military fatigues, with guns drawn, approached the plane.

When they were close enough so they could clearly hear him he shouted, "I'm sick and tired of that creep who tries to negotiate with me by phone! This is for you two down there and for all the people watching me on TV. Unless my demands are met in one hour, I'll start executing one passenger every ten minutes. To show you what that will be like, I will start now with this one!"

"Wali, don't! I know him. He was just trying to talk to me. He was not starting a revolt. Please leave him be." Ibby had forced her way past two of the hijackers and was standing right behind Wali. Wali stepped back from the open door and signaled for the purser to close it.

"How do you know this man, Tanya?"

Ibby knew that to reveal Jason's true identity would be dangerous. Wali would love to get his hands on someone as rich as Jason. "We used to live in the same town."

Wali turned to Jason. "Go sit down and don't give me any more trouble."

Other passengers weren't that lucky. When the German authorities still refused to release the three prisoners, Wali carried out his threat. After exactly one hour he executed a passenger. Ten minutes later he shot another one. This time he had the bodies dragged to the door and thrown onto the tarmac. To increase the horror of this spectacle, he personally threw the mutilated body of the flight attendant through the door as well.

The remaining passengers panicked and their screams could be heard coming from the plane. The German authorities could no longer resist and agreed to bring the three terrorists to the plane. The rest of the deal, dictated by Wali, called for half of the passengers to be released. The plane with the hijackers and the three terrorists aboard would be allowed to leave for Kazakhstan or Bulgaria, whichever country agreed to allow it to land. Wali's first choice had been the Soviet Union, but he was turned down flat.

The pilot who had been scheduled to fly from Tokyo to Hong Kong was selected to take the plane to Kazakhstan. The pilot who had been at the controls during the hijacking flew the plane to Frankfurt, but he was in no condition to carry on any further. He was sitting in the empty seat next to Jason. "Do you think the authorities in Kazakhstan will arrest that bunch of hoodlums when we land?"

"Don't know, but I sure hope so," Jason replied.

The pilot continued, "I have been wondering, do you really know that woman, Tanya? Or did she just try to save your life by saying that."

"No, I really do know her. Her real name is Ibby Kramer."

"Can I ask where you know her from?"

"Sure. Ibby is the eldest daughter of Helen and Edward Kramer. They live in the same building as I do in New York City. They live on the sixth floor and I live on the twentieth so we don't bump into each other that often. As far as I knew, Ibby left for Stanford two years ago. I hadn't seen her since."

"What in the hell would she be doing with that bunch of hijackers?"

"Beats me. She was always kind of apologetic about her father's wealth. He owns one of the finest restaurants in the city and a large part of the company that caters the international airlines flying out of JFK."

When the plane landed in Kazakhstan, a large group of heavily armed soldiers boarded the plane. They escorted the three terrorists and all the hijackers off the plane. As she passed Jason, Ibby whispered, "Please don't tell my parents."

"She must be kidding!" the pilot uttered in disbelief. "She must be totally delusional if she expects news of this not to reach her parents. Do you think they'll take them directly to jail?"

"I wouldn't bet on it," Jason replied. "With the regime here you never know. My company does not do business here. We never got a good feel as to who is in charge."

The plane left several hours later bound for Amsterdam, where the airline planned to let the passengers recover from their ordeal before continuing on to their original destination. The pilot's question remained unanswered. No one knew what happened to the hijackers.

XII

Jason was sitting at the gate of Concourse D in the departure hall of Schiphol airport when his cell phone rang. After spending a few days at the Amsterdam Schiphol Hilton he was ready to resume his trip to Hong Kong. He was expecting a call from his COO, Jerry Collins, to give him an update on what was happening at the company. He moved over to a quiet spot and answered the phone, "Hello, Jerry, what's going on?"

"This isn't Jerry, it's Wali."

Jason just about dropped his cell phone. "What?!" Then he realized it could not be Wali. "Who is this? What kind of sick joke are you trying to pull?"

"Sorry, this is not a joke. I'm Wali, and I am calling about Ibby."

"How in the hell did you get this number?"

"Simple. I called your office and told your secretary that I was a representative of the airline and I needed to get hold of you with some questions about the hijacking."

Jason realized that the caller could actually be Wali. "What about Ibby? Are all of you in jail?"

"Nope. We have lots of friends here in Kazakhstan and they broke us out of jail. But that is of no concern to you. I'm calling about your friend Ibby.

"What about her?"

"I got her to tell me who you really are."

"So?"

"Well, that makes me think you might want to spend some money to buy her from me."

"Buy? What in the hell are you talking about?"

"Call it want you want, but I am holding her. I'm willing to release her for a nice sum, and I now know you can easily afford it."

"Where is she?"

"Don't be stupid. Unless you are willing to pay what I ask you'll never find out."

During the few days Jason spent at the Schiphol Hilton he had been bothered by the question, *"What to do about Ibby?"* He assumed that eventually the true identity of Tanya would be revealed. But he couldn't get himself to tell her parents. He had decided to keep quiet until he was questioned about the hijacking.

"If she is one of you, why this?"

"Money talks. I love money much more than clingy females. The latter are a dime a dozen, but Ibby can be valuable to me. You ready to deal for her?"

Jason knew he should try to keep Wali on the line while he contacted Interpol but he had no idea how to do that. As if Wali read this mind he said, "Don't even think about contacting the police or anyone else. If you do I'll send you Ibby's head looking like that of the flight attendant. By now you know I'll have no trouble doing that."

The thought of it made Jason feel sick. A sour taste came up into his throat and he could feel the acid burning in his stomach. He made a quick decision to go along. "How much do you want, and how can I be sure you won't just take the money and disappear?"

"Five million US dollars. You can easily afford it."

"You didn't answer my question. How can I be sure you'll turn Ibby safely over to me, and where?"

"You wouldn't be so fucking rich if you weren't able to work out a deal to make sure you would get value for your money."

Despite the compliment, Jason was very uneasy about dealing with Wali. The man was a hijacker and a murderer. Jason should be trying to turn him in to the authorities. Maybe by agreeing to an exchange for Ibby, he could get to know Wali's location and give it to Interpol. But the thought of Ibby's head mutilated like he had seen on the plane made him put aside any plans of turning Wali over to the authorities.

"What do you propose?" he asked.

"Go to Thailand and check in to the Mandarin Oriental Hotel on Oriental Avenue. When you get there, wait for further instruction. Make sure you are ready to hand over ten thousand US dollars in small bills. You'll transfer the rest when you get back home and can transfer it to an account I'll give to you in Bangkok. " The phone went dead.

Jason knew if he took off for Bangkok without letting anyone know it would cause problems back in his company. Before he called Jerry Collins, he worked out what to tell him.

"Hi, Jerry. It's Jason calling."

"Feeling better after that ordeal?"

"Thanks for asking. Yes, I feel fine. But I'm not heading for Hong Kong today."

"Coming home first?"

"Not quite. I met this guy while staying at the hotel. He put me on to some fabulous ancient relics that are available in Thailand."

"Any genuine historic artifacts are strictly controlled by their government. No way can you just go there and buy them."

"I know, I know that, but this would be a black market deal."

"And you'll most likely get stuck with some phony items. Imitations are not uncommon in those countries, but they are worth next to nothing. Why go all the way over there? You can buy that stuff on the Internet."

"This is different. I know the items the guy told me about are real. He showed me lots of documentation. The stuff is real. I'd be competing against a secretive collector in Mexico City, but the guy thinks that ten thousand bucks will get me the entire collection."

"Ten thousand! That's serious money. Are you sure you want to do that?"

"Yes, I have always wanted to get my hands on something unique like that. Instruct our Hong Kong office to get me ten thousand dollars in cash, small bills. I'll be staying at the Mandarin Oriental Hotel in Bangkok."

"You're nuts. I'm sure the deal is bogus and you'll wind up losing a lot of money."

"I'll take that chance."

"I'll have it booked to your personal account. No way is the company going to pay for this stupid venture."

"Fine, I'll call you from Bangkok."

After Jason hung up he went over to the transfer desk and changed his flight.

XIII

J ason was enjoying his lunch, served outside on the terrace overlooking the river.

The desk clerk approached him. "Excuse me, sir. An envelope was just delivered for you at the desk." He held it out for Jason to take.

Jason took the envelope and hastily ripped it open. Inside was a neatly typed note. He started reading. "Go to the Pak Khlong Talat flower market. Get off at the Memorial Bridge Pier, marked Tha N6. Carry a briefcase with the ten thousand dollars in your left hand. Paste a big sticker from the Mandarin Oriental on the side of the briefcase. Wear the most colorful flowered shirt you can find. Tomorrow at nine o'clock in the morning you will be approached by a man named Tommie, who will escort you to where we will make the exchange. We will not tolerate any tricks on your part. Remember the flight attendant!"

Jason took a putt-putt out to the pier. At exactly nine o'clock someone tapped him on the shoulder.

"Hi, I'm Tommie. I'll take you up the river to the camp where your friends are waiting for you."

Tommie escorted him to one of the many open boats tied to the pier. Two men were already in the boat. When Jason and Tommie got in, the man in the back started the engine. Like all the other boats, it was powered by what looked like a big car engine with a long drive shaft sticking out the back. The propeller attached to the driveshaft did not appear to be very much below the surface of the water. Tommie and the man in front helped push off, and when the driver gave full gas they went flying up the river.

Forty minutes later they arrived at a small makeshift dock. The driver expertly steered the boat alongside. Tommie jumped out and grabbed Jason's hand to help him ashore.

When he reached out to help with the briefcase, Jason quickly declined his help. "I'll just hang onto this myself," Jason politely said.

"I was only trying to help." Tommie seemed a little disturbed by this obvious lack of trust. "Just follow me. We have a roughly ten-minute walk to the camp."

The camp was surprisingly big. It consisted of three prefab buildings that could not have been there very long. Tommie led Jason to the smallest of the three buildings, where Wali was waiting for them.

"Welcome to my vacation home," he said, laughing. "Give me that briefcase so I can count out the money."

Jason held back. "Not so fast. First I want to see that Ibby is okay."

"Fuck you, you creep! When will you get it through your fat head that *I'm* in charge here? Give me the briefcase."

The speed with which Wali counted the money indicated he was no stranger to handling cash. Jason had neglected to count the money when it arrived in neat little bundles at his hotel. *I hope my office in Hong Kong did this correctly,* he thought.

"Okay, it's all here," Wali announced. "Follow me and we'll get your young friend."

They passed two armed guards and stepped into the center building. Jason's heart stopped momentarily; he could not believe what he saw. Sitting on four mattresses scattered around the room were twelve young women. All they had on were a pair of identical bright-red panties. Most of the women looked up at them as they entered. They had a dazed look about them, as if they had been drugged. Ibby was seated in between two of the women, her head bent down.

When she finally looked up, she instantly recognized Jason. She jumped to her feet and flew into Jason's arms. "Mr. Housten, Jason, get me out of here! Please, please get me out! After we got out of jail he had me brought here. I don't understand it. Please get me out!"

Wali abruptly pulled Ibby away from Jason and threw her back onto one of the mattresses. Jason made a movement as if he was about to attack Wali but thought the better of it. Instead he took off his shirt. He bent down next to Ibby and helped her put on his shirt. He looked at the girl next to Ibby, took off his undershirt and handed it to her. He pulled Ibby to her feet and put his arms around her. Ibby started to cry and Jason tried as best he could to comfort her. Aware that she was only wearing his shirt and a pair of panties, he tried not to press her too close to his body.

Angrily, Jason confronted Wali. "What is this all about?"

"Payback, my friend. Nothing more than payback."

"What in the hell does that mean, you sick bastard?"

"Watch your language! Don't forget to whom you are speaking."

"You are no more than a murderer and a pervert."

"We do no more than your side has done for years."

"Meaning?"

"Come on, you know damn well what those Internet ads are all about. 'Beautiful Eastern European women anxious to meet Western men.' Or, better yet, 'Blond, blue-eyed beauty waiting for romance.' You know damn well all those girls are tricked into coming to the West in the hope of finding good jobs. Or in the worst cases they are kidnapped. In either case, the result is the same; they are sold as sex slaves. You all know it, but choose to do little or nothing about it.

"So now we turn the tables. We go after your women and sell them to rich men in the East. There is a big market for them in Asia, especially for the ones with blond hair and big tits. Or we use them for our own pleasure. Does that shock you?"

Jason looked around the room. He was sure most of the women spoke English and understood what was going on. He could not bear to see the pain in their faces.

"I want to take them all home. How much do you want?"

"I'd think fifty million for Cras Es Noster and another million for me personally would do fine."

Just as Jason was about to respond, shots rang out outside; thirty seconds of rapid fire. Wali turned around and headed for the door to see what was happening. Jason saw Tommie pull a military-style forty-five from under his shirt. The shot reverberated loudly inside the metal prefab. Wali dropped to the ground, blood pouring out the single hole in his right temple.

Holding the forty five aimed at the door in case any of Wali's men survived the assault, Tommie said, "Those dirty bastards. What made them think they could come to my country and get away with this?"

He opened the door and a group of women entered, carrying armfuls of clothes. They went directly to the women sitting on the mattresses and started to put on the clothes they had brought in. When they had the captured women dressed, they took them outside. Each victim was surrounded by at least three Thai women. The Thai women could not speak a word of English, but it was clear they wanted to console the victims. By gestures and hugs they made it clear that the women were safe now; that no one would hurt them. They pointed to the bodies of Wali's men. A large group of Thai men, AK-47s still slung across their shoulders, were busy loading the dead on several flatbed trailers pulled by tractors.

Tommie pulled Ibby away from Jason and handed her to one of the Thai women to make sure she was also taken care of. At first Ibby would not let go of Jason but when he realized what was happening, he urged her to go along.

Tommie turned to Jason. "We've been watching this group for quite a while. I was warned about them when they put up these buildings in this area, where most of my family still lives. When our women discovered what was going on here, they asked the men to drive them out and release the women they were holding. We knew the group was pretty heavily armed. We were just waiting for a chance to attack them.

"We got our chance when one of them approached me and offered to pay a nice sum if I would bring you here. I signaled this to my family, and an army of farmers, together with my armed putt-putt drivers, was waiting to attack them when we arrived. Those bastards were concentrating on your arrival. We caught them completely off guard and killed all of them before they had a chance to return our fire."

The sight of those women sitting almost completely naked on mattresses kept playing in front of

Jason's eyes. He was not known for having any deep concern for women and their feelings, but this struck him to the core. A feeling of rage came over him, and if Wali were not already lying dead on the floor he might have put him there.

He turned to Tommie. "I'll take care of the women. I'll hire a plane to bring them home."

Tommie told him not to worry. "We're taking them directly to a hospital in Bangkok. As we speak, the Thai authorities and Interpol are being informed. I assure you they'll receive the best of care. When they are ready, my country will make sure they are safely returned to their homes."

"I want to keep Ibby with me. There might be a question about her going home. She cooperated with Cras Es Noster, and that has to be sorted out."

"I understand. And I want to make something clear." Tommie was very serious when he continued. "Between us, there can be no misunderstanding. The members of Cras Es Noster attacked us when we arrived. They wanted to steal your money and kill us. We fought in self-defense."

"Of course," Jason replied. "I'll tell them it was lucky that I asked you to bring along a few armed men to protect me and the money."

XIV

Back in Bangkok, Jason booked a room for Ibby. But when he left her in her room she became hysterical. "I can't stay here by myself. I'm afraid! I want to stay with you."

"You're not alone; my room is right here on the same floor. I'll keep checking on you and you can come to my room whenever you want."

"I won't, I can't stay by myself. Don't you understand? I'm afraid Cras Es Noster will come after me!"

"Can't happen. Wali and his closest associates are dead. The group was decimated by what happened here in Thailand. Interpol assures me the few remaining members will be rounded up in the next couple of days. Wali was stupid enough to keep a complete record of the names and address of anyone even remotely connected to Cras Es Noster on his person. Interpol is having a field day."

"I don't care; I'm not staying alone in this room. I want to be with you."

Jason eventually reached a compromise by having the two of them move into the royal suite on the top floor. That suite consisted of two huge bedrooms, with enormous bathrooms, connected in the middle by a sitting room and separate dining room.

The next day, Jason invited Tommie to come up and visit them. Tommie could not believe that something so luxurious existed. He knew the Mandarin Oriental Hotel was one of Thailand's most luxurious hotels, but he had never imagined something as opulent as Jason's suite.

Jason wanted to reward Tommie for what he and his family had done. "I was more than willing to pay fifty million to get those girls released. I know a lot of people who would have contributed or helped me raise that sum. I think at least part of that sum should go to you and your family."

"No way, man. We didn't do it for money. No matter what people think about us, here in Thailand, we honor our women. Yes, I know about places like Pattaya Beach, but the prostitution there has to do with poverty and is not coerced. We could not allow those bastards to abuse those women and girls they kept locked up like animals. What was happening to those women had to stop!"

"I still think I should give you something."

"Not necessary. I am happy the international press gave such wide coverage to the story that a group engaged in human trafficking was killed here in Thailand and the women were set free. Several reporters did background stories on the sensitive and caring way my government took care of the victims. For once we were not portrayed as a country selling their women and young boys to tourists for sex."

After Tommie left, Jason called down to the desk and asked for the concierge. Once he got hold of the concierge he requested that the hotel contact the largest motorcycle and car dealer in town and have them send a representative to his suite.

Later that afternoon, a representative from Siam Motor World arrived. Jason wanted to order several new putt-putts for Tommie's taxi company and maybe throw in a luxury SUV for his personal use.

The salesman smiled. "Sorry, I can't sell you a tuk tuk, or as you call them, putt-putt. We don't carry them. And besides, the government won't allow them to be sold for private use."

"This would not be for private use. I want to buy them for the taxi company of a man named Tommie Boonliang. I would like for your company to arrange this for me. I am sure Siam Motors has enough influence here in Bangkok to have this done."

Ever polite, the salesman responded, "I'm sure my management would be happy to arrange that for you."

"How much would ten or fifteen new tuk tuks costs?"

"That would depend on the model. There are several different model tuk tuks in Thailand. Here in Bangkok, the so called SPG3 is the best known. I would guess it would cost at least six thousand US dollars for a tuk tuk taxi."

"That's very reasonable."

"Yes, but we will have to obtain a special license for each tuk tuk; that will cost as much as the vehicle itself."

"No matter. I want you to secure fifteen tuk tuks for Tommie Boonliang's taxi company—and don't forget the luxury SUV I mentioned.

"How long will it take to get those tuk tuks?"

"It only takes about a week to build a standard model. Special features take longer. But to obtain the licenses will take longer."

"That's okay. I'm not in any particular hurry. But I do want to make sure his tuk tuks have automatic transmission, safety belts and of course, doors. If there is such a thing as a sport version, order that. I'll give you all the details as to where to send the documentation so I can have the money transferred to Siam Motor World. Don't forget to have them include your commission."

XV

Jason was in constant contact with Ibby's parents. An army of lawyers had been enlisted to negotiate Ibby's return to the States. Her parents kept Jason informed as to the progress—actually, more about the lack of progress. In the meantime, they wanted to make sure Ibby could stay under Jason's care. He had already arranged with the Thai authorities that she would not be placed in jail. They agreed to place her under house arrest in the Mandarin Oriental Hotel until the court ruled on the US request for her extradition.

Jason was somewhat surprised by Ibby's upbeat mood. Seemingly unaware of the possible long jail sentence awaiting her on her return to the US, she pranced around the suite in a sleeping chemise. That chemise was part of the clothes Jason had bought for her when she arrived at the hotel with nothing to wear but what the Thai ladies had given her.

Seeing her bounce around in that silk chemise, which barely covered her breasts and did not reach very far below her waist, aroused some decidedly un-fatherly thoughts in Jason, which he quickly suppressed. *Don't think about it. She's Edward and Helen Kramer's daughter, much too young for you. Stop acting like a pervert. You're supposed to be taking care of her.*

But those thoughts did not go away completely. They must have settled in his subconscious. One day, in his sleep, he dreamed that a young woman's body was pressing against his and he snuggled up against her. She was tugging at the elastic band of his underpants. He woke up with a start when he felt a hand slip around his penis.

"What the hell!" He was staring into the face of Ibby, who had bent over to kiss his lips. She was completely naked. He jumped up, roughly shoving Ibby aside. "Have you gone stark raving mad?"

Ibby seemed confused. "Why are you mad? Don't you want me? I love you and you love me, too. What's wrong? Don't you want to make love?"

The shock made his erection rapidly fade and he quickly tucked his penis back into his underpants. "This is crazy. Don't you see this is terrible? I like you a lot, but I don't love you. I'm a lot older than you. I promised your parents to take care of you. You don't love me. You are dependent on me, and I assume this was some stupid way to show your gratitude. Now go back to your room; I don't want to see you again until you are fully dressed."

Ibby did not move. She sat all crouched-up on the edge of the bed. Each one of Jason's words had stung like the lash from a whip. Jason saw that maybe he was handling this situation all wrong. He ripped the sheet off the bed and carefully put it around Ibby's shoulders. He gently pulled her up and with his arm around her shoulders, led her back to her room.

When they got into the room he turned to face her, and with both hands on her shoulders he spoke to her like he was consoling a child. "I'm sorry I yelled. No I'm not mad. It was just the surprise that made me react. Again, I'm sorry I scolded you. I know you meant well, but we have to discuss our relationship. Now go take a long shower and get dressed. After lunch we can go down to the shops on the lower floor and buy some nice outfits for you. You have hardly any clothes to wear, and that must be depressing."

When they stepped out of the elevator in the main lobby, a plainclothes policewoman approached them. Speaking to Ibby, she said. "Sorry, madam, but I cannot allow you to be here. My orders are that you are to stay confined to your room."

Jason quickly intervened. "The court order mentions the Mandarin Oriental Hotel and nothing about a room. So please let us pass. We don't intend to leave the hotel premises."

The policelady took out her phone to consult with her boss. Moments later she said, "I'm very sorry. I was mistaken. Please feel free to move around the hotel, but don't step outside."

They ordered several outfits for Ibby in a small boutique tucked away among the big international brand stores that lined the lower level of the hotel. Each outfit would be custom-made. The seamstress told them they would be able to pick them up in four days. Ibby would have to come back in two days for a second measurement.

Jason selected the busy bar right off the main lobby to sit down and discuss their relationship. He had avoided opening this discussion while the two of them were alone in their suite.

They ordered drinks, and Jason was surprised to see Ibby order a double Scotch, neat, which she gulped down as soon as it arrived. When she tried to reorder, Jason stopped her. "Let's go easy on that stuff. I know you're nervous about telling me why you were on that plane, but let's just start with how you met Wali."

"It all started at the beginning of my sophomore year. I attended some rallies organized by a group who protested that the group of the richest nations in the world, known as G7, had failed to address the disproportionate distribution of wealth at their latest summit. Wali was the main speaker at these rallies, and what he said made sense to me. I went up to meet him and we got into a serious discussion about the Western nations consuming most of the world's wealth, while many raw materials were found in Africa and the East. The West just took these materials and failed to pay a fair price for them.

"The next time I met Wali, he invited me to have coffee with him. Again we got into an animated discussion, and he invited me to his apartment. Wali explained that after glasnost and the disintegration of the Soviet bloc, Stanford and other US universities admitted more students from Eastern Europe and what had been the Soviet Union. Wali managed to get into Stanford. Although many of these students received some form of financial aid, most of them had a very hard time getting by in the United States. Getting hard currency out of their countries was very difficult. Until he received a research assistantship, Wali had to live on almost nothing. He never had enough to eat and had to accept deplorable living conditions. All the while he observed the incredible wealth around him in America. He told me of his plans to organize a movement to help transfer all that excess wealth in the West to the East."

"Had he already founded Cras Es Noster by the time you met him?"

"No, that came later. By the time he founded Cras Es Noster I had already become his live-in girlfriend."

"Your father is a rich man. Tell me honestly; did you support Wali financially?"

Ibby blushed. "It was not that way."

"Come on, did you pay most of the bills?"

"Yes, but we were in love, and I did not think anything of it."

"You had no idea he might be using you until he turned on you when you got out of jail in Kazakhstan?"

Ibby did not want to answer but Jason pushed her.

"Okay, I started questioning our relationship when he started demanding money. At first they were small amounts to purchase things he needed, mostly clothing. But then he started demanding money to buy a better notebook computer and the latest model cell phone."

"Was there a change in the way he treated you?" Again, Ibby was reluctant to answer that.

Finally, she admitted that he started treating her more and more harshly.

"In what way?" Jason asked.

"Sexually." Ibby looked away as she said it. "When he moved in with me, sex was great. He was my first and he was very gentle with me. I was convinced he really cared for me and I was very much in love with him. But as time went on, things changed. He became very rough, and demanded things we had never done before. At times he hurt me. He insisted we have anal sex. I did not want to have anal sex and begged him not to try. I wanted to go back to what we had been doing when I really enjoyed having sex with him. But he forced me to have anal sex and he hurt me a lot."

"Why in the world did you stay with him?"

"I don't know. I really don't know." Ibby sat back and stared at Jason. After a while she repeated, "I really don't know." This was followed by, "You must think I'm really stupid."

Before Jason could answer, she continued. "I know you hate me for joining Cras Es Noster."

"Hate you? Of course not! You saved my life on that plane. If it wasn't for you, Wali would have blown my brains out. No, I don't hate you. During the time we have been together, locked up in this hotel, I have gotten to really like you."

"Really?"

"Yes, I mean it. I never really knew you before. Sure, I saw you often in the elevator in my building and occasionally when I visited you parents. But that was it."

"You don't think of me as a terrorist?"

"What did I do during the last couple of days to make you think that?"

"You didn't want me to make love to you. Although you said you weren't angry, I know you were."

"I was not angry! I understood what happened. Because you fell for Wali and were willing to blindly follow him, you did not like yourself very much. You hated what you had become and needed someone to love you. You needed to know that someone could love you despite what you had done. Well, I do love you. Maybe not in the way you were seeking love, but that does not make it less real. I love you more like a father loves his daughter, or a brother loves his sister. That's real love; but it does not involve sex."

"Does that mean you're going to tell me what to do, like my father always did?"

"Come on; maybe I made a wrong comparison. You're too old to be my daughter. Let's just be good friends. I'll respect you as a person. Don't worry; I won't treat you like a child. Come here, I want to give you a big hug. Hugging is not sex!"

Jason held out his arms and Ibby came over to give him a big hug. She held him a little too long and a little too tight for it to be a sisterly hug.

XVI

The telephone kept ringing. It was a little past ten in the evening and Jason had just gone to bed. Hastily, he grabbed the phone.

"Hello, who is this?"

"I'm Renold Garfield, I represent the Kramer family. I am looking for Jason Housten."

"This is Jason."

"We just received notice that Thailand has agreed to extradite Ibby Kramer. She will be put on a plane to the US within the next twenty-four hours. Most likely tomorrow afternoon your time. Mr. and Mrs. Kramer have asked that she fully cooperate with the authorities. Through diplomatic channels, we have made a request that you be allowed to escort her onto the plane. We are trying to prevent any images in the press or on TV of her being put on the plane by police. That would be extremely harmful during a trial. We are doing our utmost to prevent any public perception of her as a terrorist."

"I understand. I will definitely accompany her on the flight back home. I hope the authorities will agree to do away with the police escort. So far they have been very cooperative. They have placed her in my care, and since we strictly complied with the order of house arrest, they should be okay with me bringing her onto the plane. I am sure they won't insist on handcuffing her. Maybe I can even persuade them to do away with the police escort."

"The family greatly appreciates all you are doing for Ibby. They place a great deal of trust in you and are sure she'll be safe under your care. I too admire you for doing this, after being one of the passengers on that plane."

"Please tell her parents that was not the real Ibby. You as a lawyer must be familiar with the Stockholm syndrome."

"Of course. It will be the central part of our pleading when her case goes to trial."

"Can't you prevent the case even getting to trial?"

"That would be great, but there were too many casualties for that."

Jason decided not to wake up Ibby. He thought it would be best to wait and tell her the next day at breakfast.

Breakfast was served in their suite, and Jason was somewhat annoyed that Ibby had failed to dress and was once again wearing that same silk sleeping chemise. *Damn it. It reveals much too much.*

Jason started carefully, "You know, we can't stay in this hotel forever."

"I wish," Ibby responded with a naughty little smile.

Damn it, she's still flirting with me! Jason pretended not to notice and continued. "Your family's lawyer informed me late last night that the authorities here in Thailand are sending you back home."

"Oh, shit! I don't want to go. Can't you take me to some other country? I want to stay with you. I don't care where we go, but I don't want to go home."

"The choice isn't up to me. From the beginning you knew we were only allowed to stay in this hotel until Thailand agreed to send you back home. Ibby, be realistic. There will be a trial; we can't just forget what happened. Your parents have hired top lawyers to defend you, but there will be a trial."

Ibby pushed back her chair and ran to her room. Jason followed her. Ibby was lying facedown on the bed, crying. Jason sat down next to her and softly stroked her hair.

"Ibby, it will all turn out all right. The lawyers will explain what happened. It's not that unusual. You'll have a chance to explain."

"They won't care! Remember Patty Hearst? I know what they did to her. They did not understand or care."

"They'll understand now. President Jimmy Carter commuted her sentence and President Bill Clinton even pardoned her."

"They'll lock me up forever! I did a really bad thing. That flight attendant did not deserve to die."

"You did not kill her!"

"I did not stop it. I can't forget the sight of her lying on the tarmac. I could have pushed Wali out the open door."

"Now you're being totally unreasonable. Wali was not alone. That crazy guy they called Danat would have slit your throat with his box cutter."

Ibby sat up and Jason let her bury her head in his arms until she stopped crying. Finally she straightened herself out and sat erect, facing Jason. "Will you be coming with me to the States?"

"Yes, I'll come with you. We'll try to have them agree to let me bring you onto the plane. The two of us will travel together. Your lawyer stressed that we look relieved. It must be clear you are returning willingly."

"I'll try my best. Will my parents be there to meet us when we land?"

"I assume so. I'll go down to see if we can pick up your new clothes one day early. You should wear one of those new outfits. You look great in them and it will make you feel better. We don't have much time left; I'd better go now to check."

XVII

The people in the boutique were very accommodating and assured Jason that if he came back in two hours, everything would be finished.

Before returning to the suite, Jason stopped by the reception desk to ask them to prepare his bill for checkout. While he was waiting to be helped there was a huge commotion outside the hotel. Within minutes Jason heard loud sirens, as fire trucks and police cars descended on the hotel. Jason's first thoughts were that the place must be on fire. But the fire alarm did not go off. One of the desk clerks went out to see what appended. When he returned he headed straight for the manager's office. Moments later the hotel manager emerged and approached Jason.

"Mister Housten?"

"Yes, that's me."

"Sir, would you please step into my office?"

Jason was curious as to what was going on and quickly followed the man into his office.

The manager looked pale and appeared to be shaking when he said, "Sir, have a seat. Please sit down."

Now Jason became really worried. *Is this a police raid to arrest Ibby and drag her to the airport?*

Before Jason could ask a question the manager said, "I'm sorry, sir, but I have to tell you someone jumped from your suite. From the balcony. I fear it might be your lady friend."

It did not fully register with Jason. "Someone did what?"

"She jumped from your balcony and the police have asked that you come outside to identify her."

It was as if the world had exploded around him. His mind raced at warp speed. *This cannot be true; it can't be Ibby. I should never have left her alone. I knew she was upset; I should have stayed with her!*

Jason did not hear the manager say, "Please, sir, follow me."

He did not react until the man gently took him by the arm. "Please, sir, we need you to identify her."

When they reached the terrace Jason saw the white sheet covering the body and he pulled back. The medical officer in charge stepped forward. "If you'll let me, sir, I'll help you."

He firmly took Jason's arm and guided him to the white sheet. When they stood next to the sheet he held Jason tightly while another medic pulled back the sheet.

Jason let out a screech. "It's Ibby!"

He turned away quickly and ran for the nearby river, where he threw up all over himself. In a daze he stepped into the river and the two medics who had raced after him had to pull him out of the water. They wrapped a blanket around him and slowly guided him back into the hotel. From there the hotel staff took over. They did not take him to his suite. That would have been mentally too much for him. He was brought into another room and the hotel doctor was summoned. The doctor arrived, followed by two nurses. They got Jason out of his wet clothes and put him in a hot shower. Clean clothes were fetched from his suite. They asked if Jason felt well enough to talk to the police.

XVIII

"Excuse me, sir, are you feeling all right?"
The flight attendant reached over and shook Jason very gently by the shoulder. Jason did not respond and he tried again. "Are you okay, sir?"

With a shudder, Jason woke up. His forehead was covered with sweat. He realized he had been having a nightmare and was embarrassed. The passengers seated around him in the first-class cabin were all looking at him. He straightened himself up in his seat. "Yes, I'm fine, thank you."

The flight attendant realized his embarrassment. "You'll be more comfortable in the lounge. Follow me, and I'll pour you a drink."

When they got to the lounge, the flight attendant pointed to the two seats at the far end. Jason went over to sit down, and the flight attendant sat down in the seat next to him. "Sorry I woke you up, but I had to warn you that you were murmuring in your sleep."

Jason was mortified. "I was murmuring in my sleep?"

"Don't worry. It wasn't a big deal. It was barely audible; no one understood what you said. I know you have been under a lot of stress lately; sit here and relax for a while."

Jason looked at the flight attendant. "What are you talking about?"

"It's been on TV in a lot of countries and many newspapers covered the story for days. When I saw your name on the manifest, I knew it was you. They did not have any recent pictures of you and the old shots of you unveiling one of your very first computers were not very clear. But I knew immediately it was you. You are a hero for rescuing those girls!"

"I did not rescue anyone. The Thai people did."

"Not according to the news agencies. After your plane was hijacked, you tracked down the hijackers, who had escaped from jail in Kazakhstan. You learned they were involved in human trafficking and holding women in their so-called pleasure camp in Thailand. You notified the Thai authorities and led the raid that freed the women. Don't be so modest. Of course you are a hero."

"All that was in the news?"

"Yes. They also reported there was an American girl in that camp. You offered to escort her home, but unfortunately she committed suicide before you got her on the plane."

"And this story has been on TV and in the newspapers?"

"Yes, it was given wide coverage. It followed right on the heels of the hijacking of the plane and, of course, the story of the hijackers escaping from prison in Kazakhstan. The public got quite involved, and the German government was highly criticized for giving up those three prisoners."

"Did anyone give any interviews?"

"The press tried to find you, but your spokesperson said you had secretly returned to the US on a private plane. No one has any idea you're on this plane. Unless, of course, you have been in contact with your family. If I may ask, where have you been hiding?"

"The police never detained me. They knew I was at the reception desk at the time the girl jumped from the balcony. I called a friend of mine who owns a taxi company in Bangkok. He came immediately and snuck me out of the hotel. I spent the next week and a half with his relatives in the country."

"Well, they did an excellent job in protecting your privacy."

"They are great people. They hovered over me twenty-four seven. No outside contact, TV, or newspapers. They even took away my cell phone after I had called my office and made a few more personal calls. My friend stayed with me all that time. He brought me to the airport less than two hours before my plane left."

"You were lucky to get a seat."

"I had to go through an extra security check because I booked a one-way ticket just before departure. But you mentioned my spokesperson?"

"Yeah, he was on TV all the time and every newspaper you can imagine carried a quote from him."

"Did you catch his name?"

"You don't know? It was Renold Garfield."

XIX

After clearing customs, Jason grabbed his suitcase and headed for the large double doors that opened into the area where a large crowd was waiting to meet the passengers.

Before leaving Bangkok, Jason had contacted Jerry Collins and given him his arrival time and Delta flight number. Jerry told him Hawkins was on vacation. He told Jason he would arrange a limo to pick him up. He was sure the limo company would be able to look up the arrival gate at JFK and the exact time the plane was scheduled to land.

Jason looked around, hoping to spot his limo driver when he heard. "Jason, Jason, over here, honey."

At first Jason did not realize it was for him; he did not expect anyone. But then he saw the tall blonde pushing through the crowd and heading straight for him.

It was Kristy Holoway, his 'when he was in town' live-in girlfriend.

"Welcome home." She threw her arms around him. "I'm so glad you're home. I was so worried about you and I missed you so much."

Jason tried to respond but her lips were covering his mouth. After she finally let go of him he managed to ask, "How did you know I'd be on the plane?"

"I've been in constant contact with Jerry. I've been praying you'd call me to tell me you were all right. I've been worried sick since the moment I heard your plane was hijacked." She gave Jason another tight squeeze, followed by a long kiss.

Jason finally managed to say, "I asked Jerry to send a limo to pick me up; we should try to locate the driver."

"I already did. He's waiting for us at the exit."

The limo was traveling along the Van Wyck Expressway. The driver had been bucking heavy traffic, but they were almost at the Triborough Bridge. Kristy and been talking non-stop since they'd left JFK. She had closely followed Renold Garfield's press conferences and was impressed by Jason's heroism. "Tell me about the raid; were you scared?"

Jason tried to brush it off. "It wasn't like that. There were a lot of Thai people involved."

Kristy turned serious. "I was hurt because you never contacted me. I could not call you because you never gave me the number of the business phone you use exclusively overseas. I repeatedly asked Jerry to have you call me, but you never did. And he refused to give me your business phone number."

Jason became a little offensive. "I swear he never mentioned it! You know very well he could not give you that phone number. Besides our private cell phones, he and I have a business cell phone. The number is secret. Only he and I and our private secretaries have the number. Well, that's not totally true; it is also given out on a need-to-know basis to a few top executive in the company. I'd be on the phone all day if we did not do this. I never take my personal phone with me when I'm on a business trip. People call my secretary and leave messages."

Kristy realized she was getting nowhere with that subject and decided to drop it. She switched to asking more details about the hijacking and his pursuit of the criminals. She attributed Jason's evasive responses to his reluctance to recall the events.

It was late by the time they got to the apartment, and Jason was dead-tired after the long flight. They had a few stiff drinks and went to bed. Kristy knew the long flight had tired Jason, but his silence and sullen mood troubled her. She snuggled her naked body up against him and when he did not respond to her touch, she wrapped her long legs around him. "Honey, what's the matter? What is troubling you? Is there something you can't tell me? Did you meet another woman you like better? Am I about to get the heave-ho?"

The answer she feared never came. Jason buried his face between her breasts and burst out crying. Kristy had never seen Jason cry or shown any sign of weakness. In amazement she asked, "Honey, what is it? What happened? Did they hurt you?"

This time Jason did not hold back. "It didn't happen that way. I don't even know that man Renold. His story is a lie. It did not happen that way!"

"What did not happen? We all heard about the hijacking of the plane. Mr. Garfield could not have made that up. I saw it on TV. They covered everything, including those dead bodies on the tarmac."

"Yes. All that did happen, but there is much more."

She pulled his head back into her chest and slowly let her fingers glide through his hair. "Want to tell me about it?"

Jason did not answer right away. He let Kristy cuddle him for a while. It was as if he was considering how much he could trust her. Then he made up his mind and sat up straight. Kristy looked at his sad face and knew enough not to ask any more questions, but to just let him talk. She pulled the sheet around her to cover her naked body and waited for what was coming.

"It all started when this maniac called Danat came bursting into first class." Jason continued to give a detailed account of what happened on the plane. He described how he recognized Ibby and how she saved his life. He went on to describe how he had attempted to 'buy' Ibby from Wali. He praised Tommie and his family for executing the raid. He was sure if they had not shown up when they had, Wali would have killed him. He went into great detail describing Wali and how cruel the man was. He did not touch on anything that transpired between Ibby and him during the time they were together in the hotel. He described the horror of looking at her broken body lying on the hotel terrace in much the same way as he did seeing the bloody body of the flight attendant.

When he finished, he got up and sat down in the living room. Kristy pulled on a robe and followed. She poured him another drink and sat down opposite him in one of the big leather chairs.

"All those events involved a lot more people. Parts will or have already leaked out. How will we handle what they say that directly conflicts with what this man Garfield has said?"

"We?"

"Damn it! Stop pushing me away. Your whole world is you and them. It does not always have to be that way. Try thinking *we* for a change. In this case, you and me. Try getting it into your stupid head that I like you more than just a little. I love you! Whatever happens, I'm going to share it with you. We'll have to let the truth come out, and you'll have to openly contradict what Garfield said."

"He was only trying to protect Ibby and her family."

"I get that. You can claim she joined Cras Es Noster against her will. It's okay for you to make up a lie to protect her and her family. Tell people she confided in you that that monster Wali threatened to kill her family if she did not follow him. People will understand she fell in love with that handsome bastard; he took advantage of a naïve young girl and coerced her into doing things against her will. They'll be on her side and not condemn her for participating in the hijacking."

Jason considered what Kristy was saying, but first he responded to something she said before. "Did you say you love me?"

"Yes, I did. It's an emotion you don't understand!"

"I think I learned."

"You think you learned? What the hell does that mean?" Kristy asked. She was mad. "It means a hell of a lot more than pressing you against my naked tits when you feel bad. When you hurt, I hurt. I don't think you have a clue."

Jason looked at Kristy in a strange way. Suddenly, it hit her. "Oh, shit. That girl was in love with you and you feel guilty that she jumped off that balcony!"

Kristy did not wait for a response from Jason before she added, "You didn't screw around with that naïve young girl, did you?"

"Damn it. I did not touch her!" Jason's response was angry. "Yes she was in love with me, but I swear I never touched her."

"What makes you think she was in love with you? Why in the world would she fall for you right after her horrible affair with Wali? After the way he treated her I would think she would want to stay away from men for quite a while."

"Yeah, that would have been a normal reaction. Especially after he put her in that camp among the other girls and let his men have their way with her."

"You put that nice and gently. You must have had some feeling for the kid if you can't just say he let them fuck her."

"Stop it! She didn't deserve what they did to her. None of those girls deserved it! Those bastards were animals. It was horrible. I can't get it out of my mind. Those poor women sitting naked on a bunch of mattresses, knowing they could be abused at any time by that filth."

Kristy realized she had gone a little too far in her choice of words. She went over to Jason and slid next to him in the big leather chair.

"Sorry, I did not mean to be so crude. Yes, it's horrible what happened to those women. You're right; no one deserves that. I can't imagine what that would be like. But what makes you think that girl was in love with you?"

"Okay, if you must know, she crawled in bed with me while I was sleeping. And it wasn't because she was scared! She was naked, and thought it was all right because she and I were in love."

"Oh boy. That's not very subtle, is it? How did you react?"

"At first I was hopping mad, but then I tried to defuse the situation. I think I understood why she needed me to love her. I was dealing with a young woman with a very bad sense of reality. After all the things she went through, she clearly did not like herself very much. She needed someone to show her she was worth liking; she desperately needed someone to love her."

"Did you have any clues before she got into bed with you?'

"Yes. She pranced around the suite in a sheer sleeping chemise. She had a nice body and I have to admit, it provoked some inappropriate thoughts. I suppressed those thoughts. In retrospect, I should have realized she was coming on to me. I should have stopped it right then and there."

"You shouldn't blame yourself for having some, what you called, inappropriate thoughts. You might not have much consideration for the feelings of others, but you are human. Guys react that way when they see young women in skimpy clothes, especially when the girl has a nice body. But you'll have to go and see her parents."

"I can't. Not yet, anyway."

"Oh yes you can, and it can't wait. I'll be with you. You won't have to face them alone."

"How can I tell them the truth? That she joined the terrorists."

"If you liked the girl, you won't. You'll stick to the story I proposed. She was coerced by Wali into joining Cras Es Noster and participating in the hijacking. He threatened to kill her family if she didn't. There is some truth to it. She did save your life! If anything, that makes her my hero."

"You'll come with me?"

"I said I would. You're not alone in this. I'll call them first thing in the morning and arrange for us to meet with them in their apartment."

Jason responded halfheartedly, "Okay, I guess I have to face them sooner or later. I dread having them ask me about her fall. I can't face having to describe the scene on the terrace, what it was like seeing her mangled body."

"There is absolutely no reason why you should have to go into those details. That would be cruel. But we will have to straighten out parts of the story."

For the first time in their relationship, Kristy showed her practical side. "Parts of the story will leak out, if they haven't already. Among others, they'll interview the pilot and he'll relate what he saw. You'll have to have a press conference and tell the true story but you can stick to the part that Ibby, alias Tanya, was being coerced into participating. If they bring up the Stockholm syndrome and try drawing a parallel to the Patty Hearst case, just tell them point-blank, 'It ain't so.'"

"What about that guy Renold Garfield and the information he gave out?"

"Shouldn't be a problem. His only goal must have been protecting Ibby. I am sure he'll be glad to join us and explain it was difficult getting correct information out of Thailand and that he could not reach you."

"I'll call my secretary or Jerry and ask them to organize a press conference."

"You'll do no such thing. This is not a company matter. This is strictly private and *I'll* arrange a press conference."

XX

Kristy arranged the press conference to be held the following Friday in Jason's apartment. To ensure there would be enough room for all the attendants, she specified it would be by invitation only.

Jason was flanked by Ibby's parents and Renold Garfield when he made his opening statement. Kristy stayed in the background. He started by apologizing for being inaccessible to the press in the days following Ibby's suicide. He explained he felt responsible for her. After all, the authorities in Thailand had released her into his care. He should have better judged her mental condition while spending those days with her in the hotel awaiting extradition. He related how the two of them had discussed all the details of the way Wali had coerced her. He stressed that he had assured her there was nothing to fear. Once back in the States she could explain everything. He told her the whole extradition thing was just a formality.

When Jason got to the part where Wali offered to sell Ibby to him, there were audible gasps among the members of the press. Hands flew up to ask questions. Jason waved them off. "I promise to answer all your questions after I tell you about my friend Tommie Boonliang. If there are any heroes in this tragic story it would have to be Tommie and his family. They rescued those women and deserve all the credit. I want to make sure you tell the world about Tommie and his relatives."

True to his promise, Jason did not evade any questions. He even sat down with a few members of the press and gave them a short private interview. In the meantime, Kristy took care of Ibby's parents and Renold Garfield.

After all the microphones and recording devices had been packed away and the last guests had left the apartment, Jason plopped down on the couch. He was exhausted. Kristy sat down next to him. "Feel better now that you got it all off your chest?"

"Uh-huh. Thanks for helping me do this. I really didn't know how to handle this."

"You don't have to be an expert at everything. I'm glad you finally let me do something for you."

"You know what still bothers me?"

"No, what?"

"Those thoughts I could not suppress when Ibby's chemise revealed too much. That makes me not much better than that pervert Wali."

Kristy giggled, "Cut it out! You're just a healthy male. Men can't help following their penis. I know it's my body and not my brains you're after. Don't go righteous on me now."

Jason continued in a thoughtful vein, "Seriously, talking about Wali; he was not all wrong. We in the West do take more than a fair share of the world's resources, and it is fair to say that in the past, and even now, we screw Africa and the East. We're not so nice when it comes to our neighbors in South America either."

Kristy interrupted him, "But what Wali did and stood for was evil. You cannot combat wrong by doing evil things."

"So you're saying we can decide what is permissible in fighting the wrongs of the world?"

"I'm not saying that. Not everything is black and white; there is a lot of grey area. But one thing is clear. You can't do evil things and hide under the banner of righting a wrong. Yes, we have the right and duty to say, 'Do no evil.'"

"Wrong quote. It is 'hear no evil, see no evil, speak no evil.'"

"I know that, but I'm adding do no evil."

"How would you portray that?"

"Well, the fourth monkey will shake his finger, signaling don't do it. I would amend the saying. For me it should be, 'Hear no evil. See no evil. Speak no evil. Do no evil.' Sets with four monkeys already exist. In those sets the fourth monkey covers his penis. To me that is silly. Using your penis is not inherently evil. It can be, but I don't think it should be the fourth 'do not.' I like my idea with the monkey admonishing you by shaking his finger at you.

"I have a friend who casts small bronze figurines. I'll ask her to make one with the monkey pointing an admonishing finger. I'll have her put the monkey on a base labeled DO NO EVIL. I'll give it to you so you can keep it on your desk and always remember what real evil can do."

"Since when are you the great philosopher?"

"I'm not, but I did take a philosophy class at Barnard."

That caught Jason's attention. "You went to Barnard?"

"Yes, I did, but I had to drop out after my sophomore year."

"Why. Did you fail?"

"No, it wasn't that. As a matter of fact, I did very well. No, I had to quit because we needed the money. My mom got sick and had to stop working and Dad could no longer afford the doctors' bills. I quit school and started modeling full-time. That helped pay the bills."

"I'm sorry. I had no idea. Is your mom okay now?"

"She died several years ago. She had colon cancer, and it eventually took her life. That was quite a while ago. My dad has since remarried and lives in Florida now."

"Why did you never mention that you attended Barnard?"

"Because I knew you like women with empty heads and sexy bodies. All you want is that we are good-looking and willing to spread our legs for you."

"Bang! That's a shot in the head. Are you that bitter? Maybe I sort of deserve that, but that was a very hard blow below the belt."

"Calm down, I'm not bitter. I just thought I should put it on the line. No, I'm not bitter. I played along, didn't I?"

"Again, why?"

"You had that reputation, but the first time we dated I fell for you. Don't ask me why, but something about you got to me. I was determined not to lose you by annoying you with anything that could come close to an intelligent conversation. I decided to play dumb and not lose you."

"That makes me the dumb one, doesn't it?"

"Not really. You live for your company, and I respect that. I do wish you could have a little more interest in the people around you, but don't worry, I still love you."

Jason looked carefully at Kristy, as if he was examining her. "You're right about two things. I do like beautiful women and I love sexy bodies. But you're wrong about that third bit about empty heads. In case you never noticed, I more than just liked you. I liked you a lot, despite that so-called empty head, which now turns out to have been an act. You are the perfect package. Even though I have never admitted it to myself, I have loved you for some time now. Maybe your act wasn't so great after all."

Kristy burst out crying. Jason did not understand why. "Why in the world are you crying?"

"The guy I'm crazy about just told me he loves me. Oh my God, he loves me. He really loves me!" She threw herself in Jason's arms. He was not expecting it and they both fell on the floor where they rolled around, locked in a tight embrace.

Later that night, after they had gone to bed, Jason carefully opened the subject Kristy had not dared mention. "That apartment of yours is costing a lot of money. Not that I don't want to pay for it, but wouldn't it be better if you moved in here?"

Kristy carefully controlled her excitement. "Well, if you twist my arm, I'll consider it."

Jason failed to catch on to her teasing. "I thought that's what you wanted. You always made a fuss about having to leave when I left town."

"Now who's got an empty head? Dopey, it's what I have prayed for ever since I fell for that aloof guy named Jason Housten. Of course I'll move in!"

XXI

The waiter had just brought their lunch when Kristy caught Jason staring at her blouse. "Do you have to wear blouses and sweaters that are cut so deep?"

"Of course not, but I thought you liked a nice décolleté. I thought you did not mind me showing a little breast. I know it makes other men a little jealous."

"No, I don't like it."

"Is that why you looked so carefully at my wardrobe when I moved in a few weeks ago?"

"Now that we're more than just dating, those tight sweaters and dresses make me a little uncomfortable. Does that hurt your feelings?"

"Are you kidding? That's what girls love to hear. Just a little bit of proprietary feelings on the part of our man. It gives me a warm feeling that you want to show me off, but at the same time you don't want to share too much. Trouble is, as you saw, most of my wardrobe is that way. It's a little provocative, which helps my modeling career."

"Would you mind scaling back a little? I mean, not showing quite so much of your body?"

"I don't mind the least bit. I'm flattered, and I'm feeling more secure about your love every day. This is not controlling, this is showing me you really care about me. And best of all, you asked. You didn't try to tell me what to wear."

"I won't try to change you. I love you just the way you are. It's just that I don't like all those men staring at you, and not because you're so damn good-looking, but because you are showing so much of your body. Don't forget, you were the one who explained to me very clearly what they are thinking. You made that perfectly clear."

"That's just fine with me."

"Can I take you on a shopping spree?"

"You're such a sweetheart. Yes, please, that's so exciting! Who ever said you were cold and aloof had no idea what they were taking about."

Being uncomfortable with the way Kristy dressed wasn't the only change in Jason. Kristy saw a lot of changes in him. His obsessive attention to his company, his key characteristic, had faded. Now his focus was much more on her. Their intimacy changed radically. There was a certain hunger in the way he made love to her; something she had never felt before.

Much of this change Kristy attributed to her own attitude. She felt much surer of herself. Having never finished college, she suffered from low self-esteem.

She was convinced people, mainly men, saw her as no more than a pretty face with a sexy body. Jason had awakened a belief in herself that was not there before.

They had been living together as husband and wife for several months when Jason asked Kristy to look at something he had opened on his computer. Kristy leaned over his shoulder and saw "City Clerk Online" on the monitor.

Jason clicked on "Marriage License Online."

Kristy realized immediately what was happening. She grabbed Jason from behind and dragged him to the floor. Lying on top of him, she more said than asked, "You're asking me to marry you. Really, really, are you?"

With Kristy all over him Jason could barely manage to say, "Yes."

Abruptly, Kristy sat up. She was very serious. "Are you ready for this? This is a very serious commitment. You're not just doing this because you know I would love to be married? You know I'll stay with you regardless."

"I'm sure. I have come to realize why I avoided any commitment before. I was afraid to wind up like my mom and dad. I was so angry when they broke up. No, that's wrong; it was more a feeling of hurt. I blamed my dad, and couldn't face that one day that might be me. But you have given me something I never had. I never even knew what I was missing. I had great success in business, but a real life? No. Yes, I want to marry you."

Smiling from ear to ear Jason added, "But you have not given me your official answer."

He should not have been so glib because Kristy's answer was very physical. Before he knew it, the two of them were once again rolling over on the floor while she kept saying, "Yes, yes!" Over and over again.

Neither of them were ready for a big wedding. They dreaded having to read in the gossip columns "Business Mogul Marries Supermodel." Rather than a big society wedding, they settled on a small reception at their apartment. They invited no more than thirty relatives and friends. Jason asked his father to be his best man, and Kristy asked the head of the modeling agency she used to work for to stand up for her.

Kristy's father begged off, claiming ill health, and Jason's mother was on an expedition studying undisturbed troops of Rhesus monkeys living among Hindus in India.

When the reception broke up, Jason's father approached the newlyweds. "I have noticed Jason has lost his ridiculous obsession with his company. He is finally becoming less like me. I hope he won't make the same mistake I made. Jason, your mother and I never took time out to enjoy a real honeymoon. Kristy is a wonderful girl, and she is willing to put up with you. She deserves more than an offer to come along on a business trip."

Jason burst out laughing. "So my old man finally admits he is not perfect!"

Kristy quickly hushed him up. "Quiet, Jason, I like where this is going."

Now it was his dad's turn to laugh. "You tell him, Kristy. He's finally found someone he'll listen to. But seriously, I have this chalet in Zermatt, Switzerland, and I would love to have the two of you spend some time there. Don't worry; you'll have the place all to yourself. I'll stay away during the time you are there."

Jason was amazed. "You have a place in Zermatt? I thought it was impossible to buy property there."

"Yes, you're right. Permits are issued each year for second-home properties, and some towns, such as Zermatt and Saas-Fee, are virtually closed to non-Swiss buyers."

"Then how did you get a place there?"

"I bought it some years ago when the restrictions were less stringent. I have to admit, I wasn't shy about using my connections and throwing a large sum of money at the project. There was this wonderful place in the heart of Zermatt with a great view of the Matterhorn. I had my heart set on getting it. The price was ridiculous, but what else was there to spend my money on?"

This was a side of his father Jason had not seen before. "I thought you were so practical. All business. I never thought you would want to own a Swiss chalet. I can hear you say, 'Much too showy for me.'"

"Wait till you see it. You'll understand why I go there to catch my breath and tank up for the next round of business negotiations. I insist you take time off and go there."

This time Jason did take his father's advice. Right after Kristy's passport arrived, they were off to Switzerland.

The elderly Swiss couple Billeter greeted them with enthusiasm when they arrived in Zermatt. "Mr. Jason, we are so glad to finally meet you. Your father is so proud of you; he speaks of you often. And you, Miss Kristy, he told us you were very beautiful, and oh my, he was right."

Mr. and Mrs. Billeter lived in the chalet and were the housekeepers for Jason's father. Most of the time they acted more like the concierge at a fine hotel. They did literally everything for him. They raved about what a kind man he was. He had met them when Mr. Billeter got injured and lost his job as a ski instructor. Over the years he had been very generous to them, and they could not stop telling Jason how popular his father was in Zermatt. The couple helped make the two weeks Kristy and Jason spent in Zermatt an unforgettable experience.

What puzzled Jason were the stories Mrs. Billeter told them about the woman and her eleven-year-old daughter, Jo Jo. According to Mrs. Billeter, Jo Jo was the best young skier in Zermatt and she won many ski competitions. Her mother wasn't too bad, either. Mother and daughter spent almost every Christmas at the chalet with Noah, and he doted on the child. Mrs. Billeter assumed that Jason knew the mother and child.

Jason told Kristy he had no idea who they were and he wondered why his dad had never mentioned them. Kristy found it amusing. "Don't be such a prude. Your father is a good-looking bachelor. He'll tell you about them when he wants to. In the meantime, it is none of our damn business who he invites to his gorgeous chalet."

Once back in New York City, Jason and Kristy settled into a quiet married life, obviously enjoying each other's company. Kristy was a little disappointed when Jason announced he had to go to South Korea to help sew up a major deal. Jason didn't seem concerned about flying, but the hijacking had left Kristy a little concerned about his safety.

In the limo on the way to the airport, Jason got right back into his old routine. He pulled out the thick binder containing all the details of the negotiations with Dongbu Raon Electronics and their chief negotiator, Yun Hee Ha. According to the notes, Yun Hee Ha was a young female who went by her Western name, Lilly Park. He was to meet Lilly Park at the Commodore Hotel in Busan.

XXII

The airport in Busan was very crowded, and Jason had trouble finding a taxi to take him to his hotel. But once he arrived at The Westin Chosun, were he had stayed many times before, he was literally engulfed by the staff. He was escorted to his suite; they couldn't do enough to make him comfortable.

Early the next morning, the hotel arranged a car to take him to the Commodore Hotel for his meeting with Lilly Park.

Jason was waiting in the lobby when a young woman approached him. "Hello, I am Lilly."

Lilly's appearance surprised Jason. He had expected a business-type young woman. Lilly, wearing a very tight traditional Chinese dress, looked more like a contestant in a Miss South Korea contest.

Awkwardly, Jason stuck out his hand. "Hello, pleased to meet you."

"Please follow me. We have arranged for a conference room upstairs."

Jason followed Lilly to the central bank of elevators at the back of the lobby. True to his old form, Jason admiringly glanced at Lilly's slim figure and her long legs visible through the slit running along the side of her tight traditional dress.

Nine of the top engineers of Dongbu Raon Electronics were seated at the long conference table when Jason and Lilly entered the room. One by one, they got up to introduce themselves. When the introductions were done, Jason was asked to take a seat at the head of the table, and Lilly took the seat next to him.

For most of the day, interrupted only by a short lunch break, the engineers asked questions about Milbank's CP-1500 computer. They wanted specific changes to suit their production lines. Their main concern was that the computers could follow the process of the entire assembly line and calculate the exact time at which to insert the correct motherboard for each piece of equipment.

Jason relayed their questions to his factory and checked his own responses with Jeffrey Milkowsky, who was monitoring the meeting from his desk at the factory by an open telephone connection. At the end of the day, he promised to let them know in a couple of days if all the changes they requested were feasible, and, if so, to give them an estimate of the costs involved in making the changes.

When the meeting broke up, Lilly offered to take Jason out to dinner. Jason responded that she was the customer and he should invite her out. They agreed to meet later that evening at The Westin Chosun.

XXIII

Jason selected the Panorama Lounge for their dinner. Lilly had never eaten there, and she was delighted by the spectacular panoramic view of Haeundae Beach. The bright-red color of the Chinese dress she was wearing did even more for her figure than the pale yellow one she had worn earlier that day. Jason was aware of the critical looks they were getting from the other guests when Lilly joined him at his table. He could imagine what they were thinking.

After the waiter had taken their drink order, Lilly asked, "What a beautiful place. Have you stayed in this hotel before?"

"Yes, many times. We have many customers in South Korea, and quite a few of them are located here in Busan. Back home, people only know about Seoul. They have no idea how big Busan is."

"Busan is actually losing population. Not much, but the population is steadily going down."

"I had no idea. The factories we deal with seem to grow every year. I thought this would be reflected in the population of the city. That leads me to something I have been meaning to ask. Is it possible for me to visit your factory while I'm here in Busan?"

"Of course. I will be most happy to take you. Outside of rush hour, it is less than forty minutes from here. I will make arrangements for your visit tomorrow."

"That'll be great. It will give me a better idea of the set-up of your production lines and where we could install our computers. May I take pictures of the way you placed the robots in relation to the actual production lines?"

"That will be difficult. But of course we can discuss that when we are at the factory. "

"If I can send a few pictures to my factory it would be a great help in coming up with our proposals on how we could make the changes you requested."

"It would depend on your response to a proposal I want to make."

Jason looked at Lilly. Was she about to make a proposal that had nothing to do with business?"

"It is about a top-secret project our factory is working on. We will need some of your computers for this project but I cannot discuss this in public. Is there a more private place in this hotel where we can discuss this?"

"The hotel is always crowded, but if you don't mind, I do have a suite. We could go up there to discuss this project."

"I trust you. You cannot discuss this project with anyone. If it becomes public that would be very bad for us."

"You don't have to fear anything leaking out. My company often works with customers on secret projects that are still early in the development stage. When they intend to use our computers, they always ask for our cooperation."

It did not go entirely unnoticed when the two of them got into the elevator to go up to Jason's suite. A group of American businessmen exiting the elevator could be heard making childish comments about the couple. Jason, smelling a big business deal in addition to the one he was working on, wanted to make sure Lilly felt comfortable about telling him all about the secret project. Forgetting that he had not one but two fully stocked mini bars in his suite, he ordered a tray of drinks from room service as soon as they entered the suite.

"You didn't drink much during dinner. Will you join me in a drink while you explain the project to me?"

"Thank you, that would be nice. What are you having?"

"I'm having Scotch."

"Oh, no. No thanks. Do you have sherry?"

"Let me check what's on the tray." Jason held up two bottles. "We have a dry and a sweet cherry, which would you like?"

"I will have the sweet one please."

Jason poured their drinks and handed Lilly hers. He went to sit down on a large couch and was surprised when Lilly came to sit next to him.

She must be afraid to talk too loud about this secret project, Jason thought as he got ready to hear all about it.

Instead, Lilly said, "You and I, we could make a great pair."

This did not make any sense to Jason. "How so?"

"Well, I could be very nice to you." As she said it, Lilly closed in on Jason and sat pressed tightly to him. "I would be very nice to you if you give us what we want."

Jason had no idea where this was going but he started to doubt the existence of a secret project.

Lilly leaned into him even further and in a sultry voice said, "I will do anything you want. We will do things you only dreamed of before. All you have to do to gain complete control over me is sell us one of your UT-500 computers."

Jason pushed her away. He was angry. "You know damn well all sales of our UT-500 are controlled by the US government. They are never exported, no exceptions. What does Dongbu Raon want with a UT-500 anyway?"

"It is not for Dongbu Raon. This is much bigger than that. It is for the government."

"No such thing. If South Korea wanted a UT-500, they would approach our government. I'm sure that would not get them very far. But I'm just as sure the government of South Korea would not send you on this mission. I have no idea what you're about but I want you to get the hell out of here."

Lilly stood her ground. "Do not be so stupid, Jason. It would be good for your company. Dongbu

Raon would order a hundred or more CP-1500 computers and never bargain about price. And for you personally it would be good, too. We would show our gratitude by depositing millions in your private account. You must have one offshore."

Now Jason really showed his temper. "I said get out! If you don't leave now I'll call security." Without waiting for Lilly to respond, he grabbed her by the arm and pushed her out the door.

XXIV

J ason heard a banging noise on the door of his suite. He was on the phone with his office relating what happened with Lilly and tried to ignore it. But the banging continued and became more urgent. Jason interrupted his conversation. "Hold on a moment. Someone is at my door. I'll see who it is, be right back."

When Jason opened the door he was surprised to see a member of hotel security and two uniformed policemen standing in the hall. "What's wrong, gentlemen? Unidentified persons in the hotel?"

"No, sir," the hotel security officer said. "May we come in? These two officers would like to ask you a few questions."

"Can't that wait till later? I'm on a very important call with my office and it is getting pretty late there."

Both policemen pushed past the security officer. "Sorry, sir, you have to come with us. We have to take you to the police station for questioning."

"Question me? Are you sure you have the right person? I'm Jason Housten. I'm from the United States."

"Yes, we know, sir. Please come with us. If you object we will have to arrest you."

"Arrest me? This must be a mistake!"

"No, sir." The policemen stepped further into the suite and approached Jason, ready to arrest and handcuff him. Jason was fast enough to avoid them and grab the phone. "This is crazy! The cops are up here and they want to arrest me. Tell Jerry. That woman Lilly tried to buy a UT-500—"

The police ripped the phone out of his hands and handcuffed him before taking him to the elevator. With a policeman holding onto each arm, Jason was escorted through the lobby into a waiting police car. On the way to the police station, Jason tried to ask why he was under arrest. The policemen remained silent.

At the police station, Jason was taken into an interrogation room. He was rudely pushed onto a chair. Two men in plainclothes took seats across from him.

"Why am I here? Call the American Embassy. I want their consular service to assist me."

The older of the two men spoke. "Sir, we have a complaint from a woman named Yun Hee Ha, known to you as Lilly Park, that you assaulted and raped her last evening in your suite at The Westin Chosun Hotel."

Jason could feel the blood drain from his head and he felt faint. "That is pure nonsense. As a matter of fact, I was about to turn her in for trying to buy classified equipment."

"Her physical condition proves her claim. She was examined at Dong-A University Medical Center and the doctors found severe trauma to her anal and vaginal areas. This is consistent with her claim of being assaulted."

"She had no injuries whatsoever when I threw her out of my suite."

"So you admit that she was in your suite last night."

"Yes, she was there under the pretext of having to discuss a top-secret project for Dongbu Raon Electronics."

"In her statement there is no mention of a top-secret project. In her statement she claims to have gone to your suite to further discuss the purchase by Dongbu Raon Electronic of computers from you company. Dongbu Raon has already confirmed that she is a highly placed executive in their company and that indeed she was leading the proposed purchase of computers from your company. There was no mention of a top-secret purchase."

"Why in the hell would I jeopardize the sale of our computers to Dongbu Raon by assaulting her? And why would I throw her out of my suite if she hadn't proposed a highly illegal transaction?"

"Sir, all we have to go on is her sworn statement and the physical evidence to prove she was assaulted. You have already admitted that she was in your suite."

"That still doesn't prove that I assaulted and raped her."

"It is enough to keep you here under arrest for suspicion of having raped her. She is a respected executive in a local company, and we have no reason to doubt her claim."

"What about me? Why doesn't my word count? Is it because I'm a foreigner?"

Now the younger of the two men spoke. "Considering the excellent relations between South Korea and the United States, that is a stupid thing to say. That type of attitude will not help you. Our courts will give you a fair trial. Showing any disrespect for us or the justice you can expect in our country may reflect on the way you think about our women. That is not going to help you in this case. This lady is not some cheap little prostitute. And, even if she was, you had no right raping her."

Before locking him up, the police confiscated his wallet and cell phone.

XXV

Kristy was beyond herself. She had just gotten off the phone with Jerry Collins, who informed her that Jason had been arrested in South Korea. He told her he and Milbank's chief counsel were preparing to leave for South Korea. She begged him to take her along but he refused. She was desperately trying to book her own ticket when the phone rang.

"Hello, I'm Caroline Gallagher. You probably never heard of me, but I live with Jason's mom. Jason's dad just called us and told us Jason has been arrested in South Korea."

Kristy interrupted her. "I know. I'm trying to get there."

"That's why I called. Jason's dad is flying out and is taking me along. He also wants to take you. Do you have a valid passport?"

"Yes."

"Good. That's all you need. We don't need visas. Arrangements are being made for his plane to pick me up tomorrow. He says we can be at Westchester

County Airport late tomorrow afternoon to pick you up. He expects fewer delays flying in and out of Westchester than Teterboro in New Jersey, which would have been more convenient for you. Can you be there?"

"Yes!" Kristy almost screamed her answer into the phone. She was so excited she did not know what else to ask.

Caroline helped. "Pack for what may turn out to be a long stay. Don't worry, there is no restriction on the number of suitcases. His dad's Boeing 787 VIP is huge, and there will only be a few of us aboard."

"Tell him thank you, thank you, thank you. I was dying to go but did not quite know how to make arrangements this quickly. This is so great what he is doing. I have only met him a few times, but he has been so kind to me."

"Noah is a nice man. He keeps close contact with me, and he has told me about you. I shouldn't tell you this, but he thinks you're very beautiful and more than his stubborn son deserves."

"Oh my! I'm blushing. I don't mind saying you sound pretty nice, too. I'm looking forward to meeting you and hearing how you know Jason's mom."

Caroline chuckled. "You may be surprised, but we'll leave that for the long plane ride to South Korea. Noah said to tell you that his pilots will be using the facilities of Million Air at Westchester Airport. When you get to the airport, ask for directions to their lounge. I'll meet you on the concierge level to bring you to our plane. If you are afraid you might get lost looking for us, call Million Air. They'll send a car to pick you up."

Always afraid of being late, Kristy arrived at the airport two hours early. She was sitting in the lounge checking her watch for the tenth time when a tall, youngish-looking woman approached her.

"Hi. You must be Kristy. I'm Caroline."

Kristy stood up to greet her. "Yes, I am Kristy. I was expecting a much older person. You did say you lived with Jason's mother, right?"

"Yes, I do. I'm not her age but I'm older than you might think. I went to school with Jason. I'm his age, so you and I are probably pretty close in age."

"You certainly don't look it."

"If I may return the compliment, Noah did not exaggerate about your looks. I had no trouble picking you out here in the crowd. By the way, this is Roger. He's our flight attendant on the plane. He'll help with your suitcases."

Noah Housten was standing at the top of the Jetway. He greeted Kristy with a big hug and reassuring words. "Don't worry. We're on the way to get him. I'm sure this is all one big mistake, and we'll have it cleared up when we get there."

Kristy wanted nothing more than to believe him but she had her doubts. *I believe in him. I love him and I'm sure I've gotten to know the real Jason during the last several months. But is he still so involved in his company that he might have done something foolish to benefit the business?*

Once everyone was comfortably seated in the large lounge adjacent to Noah's onboard office, the plane took off. Noah asked Roger to get everybody a drink and proceeded to introduce Kristy to his chief corporate counsel, Larry Martin, and Kyung-Sam Kong. Kyung-Sam Kong was an executive in Noah's company. He was a native-born Korean who went by his American name Sammy Kung. He had volunteered to come along to help translate.

Noah turned to both women, took a deep breath, and started explaining. "The situation is much more serious than I let on. Jason has been accused of rape."

Kristy sprang to her feet. "No fucking way! I know Jason. There is no fucking way he would do something like that."

Caroline was quick to agree. "She's right. Jason would never touch a woman without her consent. That can't be; they've got the wrong person!"

Noah held up his hand in a gesture to calm both women down but Kristy continued. "No way would my Jason do any such thing. They're crazy!"

Noah became a little more forceful. "Kristy, sit down. I fully agree with both you ladies, but the Korean authorities claim to have evidence. They tell us that a well-respected female executive of Dongbu Raon Electronics has filed a complaint against Jason. They faxed us a copy of her complaint, and Sammy has translated it for me. They also have a medical report indicating that she was raped. We have not been able to communicate with Jason to hear from him what really happened, but the police say he has admitted she was in his hotel suite on the night of the alleged rape."

Kristy shook her head and kept repeating to herself, "No fucking way. It just did not happen. That bitch is lying."

Caroline appeared calmer but she was no less upset. "Kristy is right. That woman is lying. We all know Jason, and this just isn't true. For some reason, that woman is lying, and we'll have to find out why."

Larry, the corporate counsel, joined the conversation. "This whole thing does not make sense. Sammy tells me he has found out Jason was working on a deal with Dongbu Raon for a considerable number of Milbank's CP-1500. That is a very big deal. Jason would never do anything to willingly mess up the deal. Noah has spoken with Jerry Collins, Milbank's COO, and he confirms that they were very close to reaching a deal."

Noah filled in what Jerry had told him. "Yeah, I spoke to Jerry. He was the first to tell me Jason had been arrested. In a later conversation, he added this interesting bit. The person heading the negotiations for Dongbu Raon is a young female named Lilly Park. He checked with the people involved in the initial negotiations and they told him it is unusual to have such a young female as Lilly handle such an important deal. And here comes the interesting part. She was not actively involved in the negotiations until Dongbu Raon made some additional requests and demanded Jason personally come to Korea to continue the contract talks. And guess what? It is the very same Lilly Park who now accuses Jason of raping her. You don't have to be a genius to know that something here stinks."

The corporate counsel agreed. "I know very little about the computer industry. But Noah tells me that Milbank makes some pretty advanced computers, and even has a model the government has restricted from export. I'm willing to bet if we dig into that we'll come up with some answers as to what is going on."

To everybody's surprise, Kyung-Sam Kong said, "I can tell you what is going on. While growing up in Korea I learned all about North Korea. Their government is a filthy bunch of cheats. I bet they are behind this. I don't know how this leads to a charge of rape, but I'm sure those bastards are behind this."

Noah had not considered that angle. "You might be right. It's definitely worth pursuing. We have a branch office in Seoul. They have good government connections and should be able to help. I'll contact them right now." Having said that, he got up and disappeared into his office.

XXVI

Jason was held incommunicado. No one except for the representative from the American Consular Service had seen or spoken to him. After three days, Noah increased the pressure on the manager of his branch in Seoul. "I don't care how you do it. I want to see my son. Call every government contact you know. Ask for help. I want some action." He finally got results.

Jason was surprisingly composed when they finally allowed his father to visit him. He told Noah calmly what happened. The part about Lilly asking for delivery of a UT-500 computer fit in nicely with what Kyung-Sam Kong suspected. Jason confirmed that Lilly had told him a government was involved. Noah could not help but wonder how his son could appeared so calm after being held in a foreign jail for almost five days.

"Dad, the whole thing is a set-up. I never touched that woman. The second day I was in jail I had a visit from a man who claimed to be a lawyer you hired for me. I didn't trust him, and when I asked him a few questions about you he did not have a clue. Before I had him thrown out he did manage to give me a message. 'Agree to deliver a UT-500 to us and the rape charges will be dropped.'"

"It's becoming very clear what is going on; but how can we explain the report that there was physical evidence she was raped?"

Jason shook his head. "I haven't got the slightest idea. The only thing I might have bruised is her arm when I threw her out of my suite."

"The report contained pictures, and the injuries looked pretty bad."

"That could be, but it does not prove to me that those pictures were of Lilly."

"Of course not. The pictures only showed a woman's vital parts. But I don't think the South Korean authorities would fake the report."

"I don't think so either. But they'll have a hard time proving I raped that woman. There is no mention of sperm samples. They never tried to test my DNA. So I have to assume they haven't found traces of DNA either."

Noah was impressed. "You sound more like a lawyer than an electronics nut."

"Dad, can you pursue all these indications that the North Korean government is behind this? Everything points that way. Lilly mentioned a government, and the South Korean government would never use this method to get a UT-500."

"My office in Seoul has already obtained information that the police are looking into this. This is unofficial. The good news is that the South Koreans are taking your version of what happened seriously. They can't dismiss the woman's complaint, but they are not dismissing your allegations, either. The initial investigation is in the hands of the police, but my office has contacted the National Intelligence Service. We are pretty sure that the NIS will launch their own investigation."

Before Noah left, Jason wanted him to know, "When they locked me up I did not panic. I know my dad and my wife. I know you trust me and you would come and get me out of here. Neither of you gives up easily. Both of you are fierce fighters. I just knew you would get me out of this mess."

Noah gave is son a big hug. "We won't let you down."

XXVII

Caroline and Kristy spent a lot of time patiently sitting around the hotel. There was little for them to do while Noah was busy trying to get people to look into the possibility of North Korea's involvement in Lilly's demand for a UT-500.

They were having lunch in the coffee shop when Kristy said, "I have noticed that when you and Noah discuss Jason's mother, you refer to her as Mom. Jason never mentioned he had a sister, or half-sister."

"Yes, I call her Mom, but I'm certainly not Jason's sister, or even half-sister. Mrs. Housten took me in while I was in high school. My mother died when I was pretty young and I did not get along with my stepfather. As I mentioned before, Jason and I were classmates."

"And you're still living with Mrs. Housten?"

"Yes. After my divorce, my daughter, Josephine, and I moved back in with her."

"Sorry. I did not mean to pry. I did not know you were divorced."

"Oh, don't worry. I don't mind talking about that mistake."

"Mistake? That sounds intriguing."

"Not very intriguing. Just call it stupid on my part. Good thing Noah came to my rescue."

"Rescue, wow! Now you've got me curious."

"Okay, I might as well tell you about it. When my stepfather passed away, he left his entire estate to me. He was the chairman and majority shareholder of our local bank. Rather than sell those shares I decided to hold onto them and assume the chairmanship of the bank. Of course I was much too young and inexperienced, but I had the full support of the board. They had feared I would sell my shares to one of the national banks. That would have ended their hold on local matters.

"A young, rich bank chairman was easy prey for an ambitious young real estate agent. He was very handsome and courted me aggressively. Against Mom's advice, I married the scoundrel. Besides trying to get control of my money and the bank, he was abusive. Mom stepped in and called on Noah for help. She convinced him the situation was not good for his granddaughter's welfare. Noah, true to form, chased the young man out of town with his tail between his legs."

"Wait a minute. His granddaughter? But you're not his daughter."

"Oops. You're right. You might as well know. Josephine is Jason's daughter."

"Does he know that?"

"No. I never told him."

"Why on earth not?"

"We went together during high school and a long time after that. We were not promiscuous, but this happened. Jason was not ready to get married, and I was not about to make him marry me out of obligation. Mentally, he was not ready for the commitment of marriage, but I knew he would have married me if I told him I was expecting his child. That would have been a bad beginning for us, and probably for the child."

"You say the two of you had a relationship a long time after high school. I'm not the other woman, am I?"

"Goodness no. Josephine is almost twelve. By the time you met Jason, I was already divorced from that creep. No, you are certainly not the other woman. But I must say you did something no one else managed to do."

"What was that?"

"Jason is a great guy. I wouldn't have gone with him for all those years if he wasn't. But he did have a problem; somehow he could not get too deeply involved in other peoples' feelings. Not that he did not care, but his brain was always pushing him to create the products he envisioned, and then he had to make them into a success. You got through to him and showed him there is another dimension to life."

"Do you mind that I'm married to Jason?"

"Tough questions. I guess I'm a little ambivalent about it. I have to admit, I still have a soft spot for

Jason. But Noah has told me a lot about you. He thinks you are great and are perfect for Jason. He says you make Jason very happy, and I welcome that. So, to answer your question, I'm okay with it. If he were married to some bitch I might have tried to interfere."

"Wait a minute! Josephine . . . Jo Jo. You are the one who spends Christmas with Noah at his chalet! That solves the mystery. Jason was trying to figure out who you were."

"Yes. It's a great place, and Noah dotes on his granddaughter. He has always called her Jo Jo. He's the only one she lets call her that. He spoils her rotten, and I often have to put a stop to it."

"At one point, you'll have to tell Jason."

"Yes, and I'm hoping you'll be my ally and help smooth the way."

Kristy did not know if she dared put a condition on helping with this delicate matter. But she felt this gave her a chance to protect Jason's rights and at the same time, fulfill a selfish wish for herself. "I'll help, but only if you let Jason become part of Josephine's life and let me be a sort of aunt."

"I do want Josephine to know her father and for you to become part of her support group."

"That would be so great! Except for my father, I have no family of my own, and he and I have hardly any contact. I can't have children of my own. I was diagnosed with ovarian cancer and I had a hysterectomy when I was twenty-five."

"Oh, gee. I'm sorry to hear that. Don't worry; if Jason agrees, I'll share. Noah has had that child all to himself much too long. It's time for some other influence. She's about to enter the difficult teens."

Their very personal conversation was interrupted by Noah, who brought good news. "One of our contacts at the NIS has put us in contact with a gentleman named Young Ja Cho. According to their records, he is Lilly's grandfather. Mr. Young Ja Cho is eighty years old and was a member of Korea's Agency for National Security Planning the ANCP, later called the ANSP. He was dismissed from the agency when it was purged, due to unauthorized political activities. Rumor has it that during his heyday at the agency, Young Ja Cho was not averse to chasing pretty women.

"He was instrumental in helping his son, who everybody calls Jimmy, escape from North Korea. As a young soldier, Jimmy was captured on the border and held in North Korea for more than twenty years. By the time he escaped back to the South he was married and had five children. Young Ja Cho helped the entire family escape. For safety, they all assumed new names.

"As you can imagine, Mr. Young Ja Cho is extremely anti-North Korea, but he is also very proud of his granddaughter, Lilly, and furious about what she claims happened to her. Nevertheless, we think Young Ja Cho can put us in contact with Lilly. Officially, she is sticking to her story, but with the help of her violent anti-North Korea grandfather, we might get a different story out of her."

XXVIII

Noah's hopes were dashed when he met Young Ja Cho. Young Ja Cho was a cranky old man, still bitter about his dismissal from the ANSP. He was furious about what he heard happened to his granddaughter.

Even though he was fluent in English he spoke only in Korean, and Kyung-Sam Kong had to translate. "Lilly is a beautiful girl, and your son could not keep his hands off her. The way he hurt her, he's an animal, a monster. I know, she dresses very sexy. That's her style, and maybe she should not do that. But that does not give that animal the right to attack her. Now get out of my house! I'll tell the police you tried to tamper with the witness. What do you think; that you can buy her off? No way!"

Noah had no idea what his next move should be, but when he told Caroline and Kristy they had an idea. "He mentioned Lilly had the habit of dressing very sexy. So he's not too old to notice. You'd better leave the next move to us."

Kristy knew exactly what to do. She turned to Caroline. "We have some shopping to do. I wish I still had some of my old wardrobe, but Jason did not like what I wore. No matter, the stores here will have what we need."

They wound up in a boutique featuring the type of clothes the local prostitutes would wear. After Kristy selected a very tight, short skirt and a sweater that hid very little of her breasts, she looked around for something for Caroline. She took a dress that might fit Caroline and urged her to try it on.

Caroline wanted no part of that. "No way am I wearing that!"

"If it fits, you'll damn well wear it. If you want to help Jason, you'll do it."

When Caroline came out of the dressing room, Kristy pretended to give a wolf whistle. The dress was skin-tight and left nothing to the imagination.

Kristy gave her a compliment. "Look at you! You have a fabulous figure. If I were a boy I could go for you. It's a shame to hide a body like that."

"Oh, shut up," was the only comment from Caroline.

Rather than change back into the dresses they had been wearing, they decided to return to the hotel without changing and test the effect of the clothes on men they might meet on the way. They had not figured on bumping into Jerry Collins and Noah, who were having a drink in the lobby of the hotel.

Noah looked up. "What the hell? Are you two trying to make some money on the side?"

Caroline was embarrassed and hastened to explain that this was the way they hoped to get Young Ja Cho's attention and convince him Jason did not attack Lilly. They intended to show Mr. Cho that Jason had sexy women willing to go to bed with him. There was no need to go after Lilly, no matter how sexy she looked. Noah shook his head. "Seems pretty radical to me, but it's worth a try. Nothing has worked so far."

Kristy and Caroline left to go upstairs to their rooms to change. In the elevator going up Kristy said, "Did you notice the way Jerry Collins looked at you? He could not get enough of you. The guy was literally drooling."

"Cut it out. You've embarrassed me enough for one day. I dread having to wear this dress again tomorrow when we plan to call on Mr. Cho."

"Don't be embarrassed. I know it's not your style, but you do look terrific in that dress. With a figure like yours you can get away with wearing something that tight. I'm serious! You could do worse than having Jerry Collins admire you. Usually it's me the men stare at, but he was mesmerized by you. I say that in a good way. Jerry is by no means a dirty old man. He's a good-looking bachelor used to having pretty young girls around him."

Caroline said nothing. She had not thought of herself in that way for a long time. However, she had to admit, Jerry was rather attractive. The other day when they all had dinner together, she sat next to him and they had a good conversation. He seemed interested in what she had to say.

Kyung-Sam Kong somehow talked Young Ja Cho into allowing Kristy and Caroline to visit. Dressed in their new outfits, they did not look like two women on a serious mission, but their appearance did have the effect they'd hoped for. Young Ja Cho looked them over very carefully and realized these two women were every bit as sexy as his granddaughter.

After a while, he even switched to English, bypassing Kyung-Sam Kong when he spoke to the women. "I never expected that man's wife to be so pretty, and his first wife is very pretty too. It makes we wonder why he would do such a thing." Turning to Kristy he added, "Does it not make you very angry that he attacked Lilly? Do you not feel angry?"

Kristy's answer was blunt. Sitting directly opposite Young Ja Cho and giving him a great view of her breasts she said, "No! Because he did not do it. Now I ask you. Did you ever consider that your granddaughter could be in grave danger? You, of all people, know about North Korea. We are sure they are trying to get their hands on an advanced computer made by my husband's company. Lilly is being forced to cooperate."

Young Ja Cho was stunned. He had never heard Jason's version of what happened and that Lilly asked for delivery of a UT-500.

Kristy continued, "Did you ever stop to consider if Lilly was really qualified to have such a high position in an electronics company? And have you ever asked yourself who is behind Dongbu Raon? Who really owns that company?"

Young Ja Cho took his eyes off Kristy's partially exposed breasts. He was visibly shaken. "You mean Lilly never was raped?"

Caroline jumped in. "We know she was never raped. We don't think Lilly voluntarily cooperated. Someone or some organization set up this rape story to force Jason into delivering a UT-500. They went so far as to send someone to see Jason while he was in police custody. That person was sent to tell him the rape charges would be dropped if he agreed to deliver a UT-500."

"I can ask Lilly. I'm her grandfather, she respects me. She'll talk to me."

Caroline held up her hand as if to say not so fast. "Mr. Cho, please be careful. If what we suspect is true, she could be in danger. They know your reputation; if they find out she talked to you they might kill her."

Young Ja Cho took some time considering what they were telling him. Finally, his hatred and suspicion of the North got the upper hand. "I cannot send a message through her father, my son, Jimmy. He will not talk to her. He says she disgraced our family. He is ashamed of the fact that she is the mistress of Shin-Il Bai, the son of the founder of Dongbu Raon Electronics.

"When Shin Sa-Jang Nim died, his son took over as president of the company. He has always been known as a hard-drinking playboy. I hear he has not changed much since taking over as president. Lilly is his mistress. She has a lot of power in the company.

I have heard people refer to her as Gua-Jang, which means department head. I am very proud of her. I will tell her to contact me, but to be very careful. I will tell her no one should know about it."

Kristy was alarmed. "No! Please don't do that. Who knows? Even your son and his family might also be under pressure to cooperate. He might be angry, but she is still his daughter. We think they may all be in danger if anyone suspects they talked to her."

"Then what can I do? How can I protect her if what you suspect is true?"

"If we try to contact Lilly directly, she will refuse to talk to us. Give us some information that Lilly knows only you could know. The person who contacts her will use this as a type of password. That will assure her the message he gives her comes directly from you. You are her grandfather; you helped the family escape from the North. I bet she wishes she could secretly contact you for help."

Caroline added, "Trust us. I know you don't like the NIS but we have their complete support. Orders have come from the highest levels to investigate Dongbu Raon. Don't worry, care will be taken not to endanger either Lilly or the rest of your family. But we do need your cooperation. The NIS will contact you. An undercover agent will make the contact. Please tell them everything you know that might help.

"Tell them about people you never saw before who lately befriended members of your family. From your days in the ANSP you must remember suspicious persons who could be involved. When your son comes to visit, very carefully test his reaction when you ask questions about Dongbu Raon. Ask what he knows about what they are doing to help Lilly overcome this terrible experience. Any information you can give to the NIS will help Lilly."

Young Ja Cho chose his words carefully. "Yes, I trust you. When I first heard Lilly had been raped I was terribly angry. She is my favorite grandchild, and even though her father disagrees with me, I am very proud of her. She started as an office worker at Dongbu Raon. She worked herself up to become assistant to the president. Because she is so pretty, she caught the eye of the president's son and became his mistress. Now she is a powerful person in the company and socially, also.

"If what you say is true, she could be in danger. I really hate the North Koreans. I know they need advanced computers. They do not care what means they have to use to get them. I like you two ladies, and I do not think you would believe that Lilly asked about an advanced computer if you were not absolutely sure that Mr. Housten did not rape my Lilly."

Caroline signaled for Young Ja Cho not to get up but carefully look out the window. "That car parked across the street is not ours. We have been followed. They have been following us for days. When we leave, you have to pretend you are throwing us out. Yell in Korean for us to get the hell out of your house. Add something like; to try and seduce me will do you no good. I'll kill that bastard rapist when I get my hands on him. He hurt Lilly and you want me to help? Are you crazy?"

Young Ja Cho put on a great act when he threw them out of the house. In the car on the way back to the hotel Caroline complained that he overdid it a little. "My rear end still hurts from the push he gave me."

Kristy laughed, "Maybe he could not resist touching that nice ass of yours. Welcome to the club. Men have been 'accidently' patting me on the rear ever since I can remember."

XXIX

That evening during dinner, Kyung-Sam Kong gave all of them a lesson in Korean names. "Back home I'm called Sammy Kung, but here I'm still Kyung-Sam Kong. During the last few days, a few of you have called me Kyung, thinking that is my Korean given name. It's not, it is my family name. Sam Kong is my first name in Korean. In Korea the family name comes first and the given name comes second. Here people don't like to be addressed only by their family name. So today we visited Mr. Young Ja Cho. Next time you see him, please call him Mr. Ja Cho. He'll like that. In the hotel please call me Sammy, but outside it will be less confusing for others if you call me Sam-Kong."

Noah was surprised to hear this explanation. "I've been calling a lot of people in our Seoul office by their last name thinking that was their first name. I wonder why no one corrected me."

"Koreans are a very polite people," Sammy said. "And, if you don't mind my saying so, nobody in any of your branch offices would dare correct you."

"What do you mean? Back home in the office a lot of people call me by my first name, and they would correct me if needed."

"Yes, but it is different for the people in our branches. They don't see you very often. You might not realize it, but they are a little afraid of you."

"Afraid of me? You're kidding. Why on earth would they be afraid of me?"

"You're the big boss. Sort of a legend. The powerful billionaire who comes to visit in his private plane. They hardly get to speak to you. There are two layers of management between them and you, and their direct boss is always an American."

"Am I hearing a disguised criticism?"

"I'm an engineer and have nothing to do with running the company. But if I may say so, it would be nice if people got to know you a little better. I'm not trying to flatter you, but you are a really nice guy. All of us in the so-called top management group have gotten to know you pretty well. I think I speak for all of us when I say we not only respect you as our boss but we like you as a person. I think it would benefit the company if people down the line also got to know you better."

Larry, the senior corporate counselor, chimed in, "He's right, Noah. You are always so busy, even involved with the daily operation of the company, that you don't have time to meet the troops. I am sure they would like it, and I think you would like it, too. I'll give you an example. None of the people in our Seoul office ever sat down and had a conversation with you before now. When we visited there the other day, they not only got to talk face-to-face with the big boss, they met a real person, a worried father."

Noah interrupted him. "I think it's my duty to get involved in the details. I failed once, and the world came crashing down. Not only on me but we damn near lost the entire company."

"Even though I was not there at the time, I know all about Rotterdam and Tom Frederick."

Noah was irritated. "You're damn right you weren't there. It was a terrible mess, and I should have paid attention to what was going on."

"Maybe yes and maybe no." Before Noah could interrupt him, Larry continued. "As a lawyer, I would say you were absolutely not liable for what happened. As your friend, I understand how you feel. You blame yourself for not checking more closely on what Tom Frederick was doing."

Again Noah tried to interrupt, but Larry waved him off. "Tom Frederick was a long-time employee and had become a trusted friend. It was normal and reasonable to expect him to be honest and not cheat. The fact is, he did cheat, and he deserves the jail sentence he received. You were not obliged to hold him by the hand to ensure he acted honestly."

Noah listened to what Larry was saying. He trusted Larry; the two were close friends. He had persuaded Larry, a fraternity brother of his, to give up an appointment to a federal judgeship and join his company as chief counsel.

"I never told you this to your face but you're the most honorable man I know. You made sure the company took full responsibility for what happened in Rotterdam. You instructed your lawyers not to fight any claims, but to accept liability for the damage done by those faulty storage tanks. At the time, I was closely following the case, even though I was not involved. As your friend, I was proud of the way you handled it. I regret not having called you to tell you so. I am sorry it has taken all this time for me to realize it would have been important to do so."

Larry wasn't finished. He looked at Noah, who was visibly uncomfortable with his friend's compliments. "Having said that, I also have to add some criticism. The Rotterdam experience should not have made you lose trust in your staff. You have some damn good people working for you, and just because one person disappointed you, you don't have to double check everything. You should have more faith in your top managers. They are very capable and honest and, above all, loyal to you. Your business ethics are reflected throughout the company. It's how we operate. It's the main reason I agreed to come work for you. Sure, earning many times what I would have earned on the federal bench helped."

That last comment made everyone at the table laugh. Even Noah could not help smiling. That encouraged Larry to go on. "Noah, I suggest the next time you visit one of our branch offices, don't only closet yourself with the manager and go over the zillion reports they are required to make. Make it a little more of a social visit; involve the rest of the staff, and cut down on all those reports. Honestly, it is sometimes discouraging to have to go through all those stacks of paper you deposit on my desk on your return."

"You do read them, don't you?" Noah asked.

"Honestly, no. I have a staff of great young lawyers. They make sure I read what I have to read. They take care of the rest. I trust their judgement."

"First I get a nice compliment and that prepares me for a polite spanking?"

"No. But sometimes we worry about you. The last couple of days are the first time I have seen you when you are not in constant contact with the company. Usually you check your phone a hundred times a day for messages. E-mails have to be responded to immediately. That counts for those you send, but counts equally for those you receive. Your apartment, chalet in Switzerland, and even your airplane each have a complete office with as much communication equipment as your office at the company. Noah, you never take time off, and that is not healthy."

"Maybe the company is my life, and I enjoy being involved in everything."

Caroline objected. "Your granddaughter comes before the company. I know! When you are with her, you give her your full attention. You spoil her rotten, and she really has your number. I've never seen you say no to her."

XXX

I t took a week before they heard from the NIS.
By that time, Noah was climbing the walls, and it
took all of Larry's power of persuasion to stop him
from interfering with the investigation. Caroline had
to practically sit on Kristy to stop her from visiting
the jail and demanding to see Jason.

Finally, two NIS agents arrived at the hotel to
report on the investigation. After the usual formali-
ties, they orally gave the report. "We visited Lilly to
question her about her complaint against Mr. Jason
Housten. After we gave her the message from her
grandfather, we told her we suspected that she,
under duress from North Korea, had falsely accused
Mr. Housten of rape. At first, she strenuously denied
having any connection to North Korea, but after
long hours of interrogation, she finally told us the
truth.

"Shin-Il Bai and she traveled often to Macao to
gamble. Shin-Il Bai lost a lot of money, and rather
than admit that to his father, he frequently returned by

himself to try and win it back. By the time his father died and he became the president of the company, he had lost a fortune. He was far enough in debt that he risked losing the factory. It was at that time representatives of the North Korean government approached him. They offered to loan him the money if he would hire a gentleman named Ham-Kyu Khang to be a vice president in Dongbu Raon Electronics.

"It was this Ham-Kyu Khang who developed the plan to obtain a UT-500 for North Korea. After his arrival at Dongbu Raon, he had transferred secret, proprietary technical data about Dongbu Raon products to North Korea. He showed Shin-Il Bai and Lilly what he had done. He explained that he made sure any investigation into the transfer of this technology would, practically speaking, 'have their fingers all over it.' That, added to proof that they had received large sums of money from North Korea, would be enough to put them away for life.

"NIS was given authority to tell Lilly she would be given immunity if she testified against Ham-Kyu Khang. Lilly bargained for a suspended sentence for Shin-Il Bai, conditioned on his following a rehab program for his alcohol and gambling addiction."

The report caused major excitement among Noah's group. But one of the NIS agents quickly stopped the cheering. "When we went to arrest Ham-Kyu Khang, he had fled. We suspect that by this time he's already back in North Korea."

That worried Kristy. "How will that affect Jason's case?"

"Not at all, madam. As we speak, he is on his way to this hotel. As an apology for keeping him locked up, the police are giving him an honor escort. Shortly you will hear the sirens as they approach the hotel."

With Kristy leading, they went flying through the lobby and out the front entrance. Half an hour later, three police cars pulled up. Their sirens scared away any cars blocking the entrance. Jason stepped out of the second car. Kristy and Noah jumped all over him. Finally Jason got a chance to come up for air. With Kristy still hanging around his neck, he greeted the rest of the party. Larry and Jerry Collins got a big hug.

Caroline had been staying in the background and when Jason saw her he didn't know what to say. She stepped forward. "What about me? Don't I get a hug? " Followed laughingly with, "Don't worry, I won't bite."

"You surprised me. I hadn't expected you."

"I know. But I'm still living with your mom. When Noah called to tell us you had been arrested, she asked me to come along to get you."

Jason still seemed a little confused about Caroline's presence. But Kristy firmly took him by the arm and led him inside the hotel so all of them could further celebrate his release.

It was well past midnight when the party broke up. Noah had made arrangements with the hotel to keep Jason's suite while he was imprisoned, and Kristy had been staying in it. During the evening, Caroline had signaled Kristy that she wanted to talk to her. They excused themselves and disappeared into the lady's room. Caroline whispered, so no one else who might be in the lady's room could hear her, "I don't know how to tell Jason about Josephine. Should I just keep it from him?"

Kristy would have no part of that. "No! But now is not a good time. If you want me to I'll take the lead."

"If you're willing to do that, it would be wonderful."

"I'll do it, but I'd wait till we're back in New York. Too much emotion now to drop that bombshell on him."

"How do you think he'll take it? Will he be angry with me?"

"You were protecting him by not telling him. He can't be angry with you for getting pregnant; it takes two. No, he'd better not be angry. Maybe I sound like a weirdo, but I'm so happy you told me about Josephine. I can't have children, and I felt so guilty that I couldn't give him a child. Now he'll have a daughter. I'm so looking forward to it. It's going to be so great. Remember, you promised you'll share."

"I promise. And maybe I'm the weirdo. I really like you and wish you could have been my sister. Josephine will be lucky to have you as her aunt."

The next morning, Jason surprised everybody by saying he would like to meet with Lilly. He had received a copy of the NIS report while he was still in custody and he felt Lilly was just as much a victim as he was. They contacted her grandfather, Young Ja Cho, and he promised to arrange a meeting.

The authorities made good on NIS's promise to grant Lilly immunity. Soon after she was released, she moved in with her grandfather. The rest of the family still refused to have anything to do with her. She agreed to meet with Jason, and Young Ja Cho decided it would be best for Kristy and Caroline to come along. As he put it, "It is easier for a girl to speak in front of a girl instead of all men."

When the three of them arrived, Lilly was quietly sitting in front of the TV. Jason noted that without makeup she was not as pretty as he remembered. The large blue circles under her eyes did not help. When everybody was seated, Young Ja Cho turned off the TV. Addressing Lilly he said, "Mr. Jason asked to speak to you to tell you he is not mad at you. He thinks that you, like he, are a victim of our enemy, North Korea."

Lilly put her head down and started softly crying. Caroline jumped up and put her arm around her. "We understand; you had no choice."

Lilly looked up, tears streaming down her face. "They hurt me. They hurt me really bad."

Caroline did not understand right away. "They hit you because you failed to get the computer?"

"No, they wanted to make it look like I was raped." She closed her eyes, remembering what had happened to her. She was not sure if she should describe what happened in front of her grandfather. But he was the one who urged her to continue. "They damaged my vagina and my rear end. While two men held me, a woman repeatedly forced a huge butt plug in me. It hurt terribly, and I knew I was bleeding. They did not care how I screamed. The men turned me over and spread my legs and this woman started forcing some big instrument into my vagina. It hurt even more than my rear end. When they finished they made sure there was blood all over my panties. They put me in a car and drove me to the hospital.

"The doctors gave me some very strong pain medicine and a heavy dose of antibiotics. After they took pictures of my wounds, they called the police. The police took my statement, and the doctors made me stay the night in the hospital. I did not know they were going to hurt me like that to prove I was raped. During the night, I made up my mind to withdraw my complaint and tell the truth. But the next day. Shin-Il Bai came to the hospital and he talked me out of that. He said Han-Kyu Khang had promised he would arrange a lot of money for Dongbu Raon, and Il Bai promised to marry me if I did not withdraw the complaint. He said that as his wife, I would own half the factory and my father would be proud of me."

All of them had seen pictures of her wounds, but none of them had stopped to consider how badly she had to have been hurt to receive such injuries.

Kristy was the first to speak. "We were all so concerned with what was happening to Jason that we never considered what happened to you. At an early stage we did figure you must have been acting under duress. It was clear to us that North Korea had to be behind it. We should have known your injuries could not have been self-inflicted. As you were describing what they did to you, I could feel it. As a woman, I can't think about it. I don't know what to say; that another woman could do that to you . . . that's just beyond anything."

With Caroline's arm still tightly around her shoulders, Lilly continued, "Father was right. I should never have gone along with Il Bai's advances. I should never have agreed to become his mistress. I knew he was nothing but a weak playboy. I was too ambitious, and look what it has brought me. My father thinks I'm a whore and my country thinks I'm a traitor. I hate myself!"

Jason spoke very calmly. "I want you to know I don't hate you. I understand what happened to you. First of all, as a guy, I want to tell you a mistress is not a whore. Okay, you forgot to get the guy to marry you, but I compare you to a trophy wife, and certainly not to a prostitute. Ambitious? Not always a bad thing. And what young girl would turn down the advances of the owner's son? From what I have heard he is quite handsome, fun to be with, and of course, on top of it all, very rich. You're not a traitor. You went along with the plot in order to protect a man you like more than just a little bit. I would even hazard a guess that you were in love with him. The two of you stood to lose everything if you did not cooperate. You're a bright young lady, but Il Bai would have nothing to fall back upon. You might eventually recover; he never would. So stop the damned sulking and let's discuss what you'll do from now on."

Lilly remained silent but her grandfather spoke. "Thank you very much for those words. That was very kind of you and it speaks highly of your character. I have some information which I will share with you in the strictest confidence. While discussing with Lilly how she got into this situation, I learned that the money Shin-Il Bai received to help cover his gambling losses came from an investment company located in Singapore. I immediately contacted the NIS, and they are in the process of investigating this company. I have been invited to the local bureau of the NIS to hear the results of their investigation. If I am allowed to do so, I will let you know what they found. To me, it is obvious they'll find a link to North Korea. As I said, I will keep you informed."

Before Jason and the two women left, Young Ja Cho had one last request. "Mr. Jason, please give my apology to your father, Housten Sa-Jang Nim. I was very rude to him. Without knowing all the facts, I threw him out of my house. Now I am very embarrassed; please tell him so."

Jason assured Young Ja Cho that his father understood and that there were absolutely no hard feelings on his part.

Back at the hotel, Kristy, Caroline, and Jason told the others about the pain Lilly endured when the North Koreans inflicted the wounds intended to prove the rape. It affected Larry the most. He excused himself. When he returned, he ordered a double Scotch on the rocks. That was totally out of character for someone who never drank more than one glass of wine during dinner.

Jason told his father how embarrassed Young Ja Cho was that he had thrown him out of the house. When he relayed the apology, he added, "Funny thing, he referred to you as Housten Sa-Jang Nim. I never knew you had a Korean name."

Sammy Kung spoke up. "Not funny at all. In Korean, Sa-Jang means president. He referred to your father by his title, president. By adding Nim at the end, he showed his respect for your father. That was part of his apology."

XXXI

Noah had already called the pilots to get the plane ready and file their flight plan when Young Ja Cho arrived at the hotel.

Noah almost did not recognize him. He was dressed in a freshly pressed, slightly outdated, double-breasted, pinstriped suit. His longish gray hair combed back made him look much younger. He was literally bursting with the news he brought. "I was right! The investment company in Singapore was an operation the North Koreans maintained to direct their intelligence-gathering in Asia. When the Singapore police raided the office, they arrested six employees.

"The managers were not present. When the police went to their homes, they discovered they had fled. Two of them actually left their wife and kids behind. Like Han-Kyu Khang, they were probably in North Korea before the investigation started.

"The NIS is treating Lilly like a hero. She supplied all the details about the bank transfers of money and the Singapore investment company. This information was enough to persuade the Singapore authorities that North Korea was actually the owner of the investment company. That made them proceed with the raid on the office."

Noah inquired what would happen to the factory, Dongbu Raon. "Will the South Korean government confiscate it because Shin-Il Bai was dealing with the enemy?"

Young Ja Cho had to think about that. "I guess so. Anyway, without a sugar daddy like North Korea, he probably could not keep it running."

The businessman in Noah made him say, "Keep me informed. My son and I might be interested in a South Korean business venture. An existing company is often a safe bet. Tell Lilly we might need her as our South Korean partner."

Sammy Kung surprised everyone. "If you need a technical manager, I'm interested. I wouldn't mind living here for a while. My grandparents keep badgering me to go to Korea to find a wife. They think I'm too old to be a bachelor."

Everyone, including Young Ja Cho, laughed at that. Kristy thought about Lilly. *Not bad-looking, smart, and probably ready to leave South Korea and her bad experience behind her. Would history repeat itself? This time she should be smart enough to marry the guy.* Turning to Young Ja Cho she said, "Give my love to Lilly. I hope to meet her again, maybe next time in the States."

Noah had invited Jerry Collins to fly back to the States with them. During the long flight home, while the rest slept, Jerry spent long hours talking to Caroline. By the time they landed in America, the two of them had exchanged telephone numbers and e-mail addresses. Noah noticed but said nothing.

Jason and Kristy were the first ones to be dropped off. When they said good-bye at the airport in Westchester, the passionate embrace between Kristy and Caroline caught Jason's attention. He was not sure how to handle saying good-bye to Caroline. His dilemma was solved when Caroline turned to him and gave him a big hug followed by a kiss on both cheeks. "It's been a long while, Jason; let's make the next time shorter." Jason did not see Noah's approving smile.

The limo ride into New York City was uneventful, but because Jason and Kristy were anxious to get home it seemed to take forever. When they arrived at the apartment, they turned in early. Even though they had slept on the plane, they were still mentally exhausted from the Korean experience. By going to bed so early, and maybe due to the time change, they were both up by four in the morning. They could not fall back asleep and went into the kitchen and made some coffee.

Kristy hesitated, but then she decided the time was right. "Jason, do you love me?"

Jason looked up. "What kind of a stupid question is that? Of course I love you."

"No. I need to hear you say it. I need you to tell me how much you love me."

Jason got up, took her in his arms and after a long kiss said, "I love you so much it hurts. Now, is that better?"

"Okay, now sit down, I have something very exciting to tell you. You must have noticed that Caroline and I got along really well. We really like each other, and she told me she has a daughter."

"Did not know that. She married?"

"No, she is divorced, but she had the daughter before that. It's so exciting; she is your daughter. You are the father!"

Jason looked as if someone had just unexpectedly taken a swing at him. "No way!"

Kristy was so excited. "Yes, yes, it's true! And the good news is, Caroline wants you to become part of your daughter's life!" She was just about jumping up and down when she added, "Me, too! She'll let me share. Jason, we'll have a daughter!"

Jason still had a hard time believing what he heard. "Why didn't she tell me? And how can she be sure I'm the father?"

That made Kristy mad. "Shut up! You know damn well she never had sex with any other man while the two of you were going together. And you should know exactly when she got pregnant."

"But why keep it a secret from me?"

"I asked that too. She could not tell you. Actually, she protected you."

"What are you talking about?"

"When she came to New York City to tell you, you made it very clear you were not ready to marry her. She did not want you to marry her out of obligation. She knew you well enough to know that if she told you she was expecting a child, you would feel you had to marry her. She might have been angry, or better said, hurt and disappointed, but she knew you were an honorable person and you would feel it was your duty to marry her."

Jason let it all sink in for a while. "Then the child must be around twelve."

"Yes. She is adorable. Caroline showed me pictures. She is so cute; nah, she is beautiful. Noah says she is a young version of your mother."

"My father knows?"

"Of course. He loves that child. He admits he loves her even better than his company. And from what I hear, that means a lot."

"Are you angry that I had a child with another woman?"

"I don't know who you've been watching or listening to just now, but if it was me you wouldn't ask. I'm so happy I could scream! I can't give you a child, and that has been my biggest heartache. And now you have one, and I can be a part of it!"

XXXII

It did not surprise anyone when, less than a year after they met in South Korea, Caroline and Jerry Collins announced their engagement. During the last few months, Jerry had been commuting back and forth every weekend to visit Caroline. Caroline did not say yes right away. She'd had a bad experience the last time she accepted a proposal after a whirlwind courtship. She was afraid to make the same mistake.

She confided her doubts to Kitty. "Mom" Kitty liked Jerry and thought his love for Caroline was sincere. Caroline also discussed it with Noah, who also liked Jerry. He pointed out that, unlike her ex-husband, Jerry was definitely not after her money. He had plenty of his own. Noah assured her the guy would not come see her every weekend if he weren't nuts about her.

It was Josephine who did not go for the idea at first. She was concerned that if her mother got married, she would get to see less of her dad and Kristy. "You like them a lot, don't you?" Caroline asked.

Josephine, at thirteen, was mature for her age, and she was not afraid to express her opinion. "Yes, I love Dad. For all the years that it was just you and me I was jealous of my friends who had both a mom and dad. Not that you're not the greatest mom ever, and Granma and Granpa are the best. I love them dearly. But I wanted a father, and sometimes I even fantasized about having my own dad. Going to father-daughter dances with your grandfather is great, but it just isn't the same. And when I actually got a father, it was clear he really wanted me.

"Yes, it took Dad a little time to get used to having a daughter. But he wanted to know all about me and he really cared what I thought. We talked a lot and he took me seriously. He did not think it funny when I asked him to bring me to school so I could show my friends that I, too, had a dad. He even told me, 'I'm so sorry I was not there for you for all those years. Now I know what I missed and I understand why you wanted a dad.' It made me cry when he added, 'I hope I'm what you wished for. If not, tell me so. I owe you a lot and I'll make it up to you.' As I'm telling you this I still get tears in my eyes."

Caroline had trouble keeping her own eyes dry. "What about Kristy?" she asked.

"Kristy is very special. One of my girlfriend's parents are divorced and her father is remarried. She tells me his new wife is horrid, and she hates her. When she has to spend time with her dad, the woman treats her badly, but her father doesn't seem to notice. She tells me her mother hates her, too.

"I know you and Kristy are best friends. Will that change if you marry Jerry? I like Kristy a lot, and I know she'll never be mean to me, but will I see less of Dad and her when you're married?"

Caroline had never stopped to think how her marriage would affect Josephine. "Josephine, I feel guilty you had to ask those questions. I should have made sure that you felt secure. I should have made it very clear that if it ever came to a point where I had to choose between Jerry and you, the choice would not be difficult. You are my daughter, the most precious thing in my life. I'll always choose you no matter what. I promise you, if my marriage ever comes between you and your father and Kristy, I'll walk away from that marriage. Let me be very clear, there will be no change in the relationship between you and your dad. Nor in your relationship with Kristy, his wife and my best friend."

She might have only been thirteen, but Josephine understood the depth of her mother's commitment. She went over to Caroline and gave her a big hug. "Thanks, Mom. I knew you were the greatest, but I had to ask; it has been bothering me. I want you to be happy, too, so I promise to get to know Jerry better and to like him. I don't know if you noticed, but he has not paid much attention to me. He hardly knows me. Of course, you were the center of his attention. I understand that, but I hope that once you are married, he will have more time for me."

"Oh my God! Did you feel left out these last several months when Jerry was here?"

"Granma discussed it with me. She said when a man loves a woman, he tends to concentrate only on her. Granma said that, if he tries to win favor with the woman by being extra nice to her daughter, it sounds nice, but it should not be that way. She says you should like Jerry because you love him and not because he is nice to me. She said for me not to be jealous. She said, 'Give them a chance, your time will come.'

"Granma has a lot of faith in you. Really. She said, 'Don't worry; you'll always be number one.' I was not worried about you! I just wanted to make sure I could spend a lot of time with Dad and Kristy."

Jerry wanted a big wedding, but Caroline was not one hundred percent in favor. It was not until Kitty joined Jerry's side of the discussion and offered to have the reception at her house followed by a seated dinner at her club that Caroline agreed.

During the reception, Jason felt a little strange meeting many of his old friends again at Caroline's wedding. It did not bother Caroline one bit. She dragged Kristy along to meet everybody and introduced her as, "This is my friend Kristy, Jason's wife." From the way the two of them walked around arm in arm, people could tell she was not pretending.

Because he had been with them in South Korea, they invited Sammy Kung to the wedding. Caroline had not seen him since that time. She wanted to hear all about his life in Korea. To her surprise, he had never gone to Korea.

"You did not go to Korea? What happened?" She was astonished.

"You didn't hear? The deal did not go through.?" Now it was Sammy's turn to be surprised. "Noah and Jason's bid for the factory was rejected. They were out-bid by the ShinYong Group. Lilly was terminated."

"Do you know what became of her?"

"After Shin-Il Bai came out of rehab, the two of them got married. Noah kept in touch through Young Ja Cho. When he heard they had a tough time finding decent jobs, he bought a small hotel on Ulleungdo Island. Ulleungdo is a popular vacation resort known for good seafood. Noah had sponsored a company retreat for his Seoul office staff there. He visited them during the retreat and fell in love with the small hotel where they were staying. The hotel was not for sale, but a small annex across the street was. Noah bought it, had it completely restored, and made a bid for the hotel itself. His bid was accepted, and he hired Lilly and Il Bai to manage it for him. To no one's surprise, Young Ja Cho moved to the island to join them."

"That sounds great! Noah offered us his chalet in Switzerland for our honeymoon, but I would love to go to that Island. How do you say that? Ulyendo."

"No, no, it's Ulleungdo. I too hope to go there someday. They tell me it's a fabulous place. By the way, if you have a moment, I would like you to meet my wife."

"You're married! Good for you; your grandparents must be thrilled."

Sammy made a face at that remark and was off to find his wife. Pretty soon he returned with a tall, lanky redhead on his arm. She was not particularly pretty, but her bright-red hair gave her something special. "Caroline, I want you to meet my wife, Caitlyn McLaughlin."

Caroline did not even try to hide her surprise and quipped, "Clear you didn't go to Korea."

"No, not quite. Caitlyn and I went to school together. Same class. She got married right out of school, but by the time we met again she was divorced. We've been married for six months."

At the dinner, Jerry's younger brother, who had been his best man, was the master of ceremonies. To say his speech was bland was putting it mildly. He dwelt too long on remembering Jerry and his parents, and kept stressing how happy they would have been to see his brother finally married. *Enough already,* Noah thought as he sat waiting for his turn to speak.

Noah was a practiced speaker, and the difference between his speech and Jerry's brother's long-winded talk was striking. Noah knew just the right thing to say. He painted a beautiful picture of how two young men created a world-renowned company. They had a dream and made it come true. Everybody present knew exactly what he meant when he said the company's products were so important that some countries would go to extreme methods in an attempt to get one.

When Noah finished, Kitty rose to speak. Jerry's brother had already stood up and he quickly consulted his notes. He looked at Kitty for an explanation. She responded by, "Don't worry, I won't mess up your time schedule, but I do have something to say." With a polite little hand gesture she waved him back down and continued.

"Most of you have known me for a long time. For a while you thought of me as poor Kitty living alone in that big house with her only son. If you haven't followed closely, let me tell you what has happened to poor Kitty. Things took a one-hundred-eighty-degree turn for me when I got this fantastic daughter. This was followed by the mindboggling success of my son. Next I got the best granddaughter in the world. My ex-husband became my friend, and together we become proud grandparents. That would have been enough to make my life complete. But it did not stop there. Once again I was blessed. I got a second fantastic daughter. And if all that was not enough, here I am sitting next to my good friend and proud grandfather of our Josephine—Jo Jo, as he affectionately calls her. Hold on, folks, what are we doing here? We're welcoming a second son. Now, you can't top that! I thought it was important to tell you what happened to poor Kitty alone in that big house."

Everybody was on their feet when Kitty sat down. They clapped, stamped their feet, and the noise was beyond loud. Caroline and Kristy rushed to embrace her; Jason and Jerry were not far behind. Noah reached over and kissed her on the cheek. The photographer signaled Josephine to sit on Kitty's lap as he took picture after picture after picture.

XXXIII

K risty invited Josephine to come to New York for her sixteenth birthday. The plan called for her to introduce Josephine to the Metropolitan Museum of Art, and several of her other favorite museums in New York City. Kristy had also bought tickets to several Broadway shows. Kristy was excited now that Josephine was sixteen. This was the first visit she could do real adult things with her.

They were a few streets over from Times Square. Josephine was waiting on the sidewalk while Kristy had gone into the theater to pick up their tickets at the box office. When Kristy stepped out of the theater lobby she saw a car jump the curb and head straight for Josephine. Josephine was looking the other way and did not see the car coming. Kristy screamed: "Josephine!" Josephine did not hear her.

Kristy started running towards Josephine; she saw that the car was approaching too quickly and screamed as loud as she could, "Josephine!" She dove headlong in front of the car and her extended arms reached Josephine less than a millisecond before the car crashed into Kristy's stretched-out body.

Josephine went flying off the curb, out of harm's way. The car dragged Kristy for two more blocks before her mangled body wound up between the car's demolished front end and the shattered glass of the entrance to a coffee shop.

Within minutes, police arrived. They were just in time to intercept Josephine, who had run to the sight of the crash. She had not been aware of what exactly happened. Bystanders told her a woman coming out of the theater had pushed her out of the way of the oncoming car. It was at that point that she realized it must have been Kristy and she started running.

A female police officer grabbed the hysterical child; it was all she could do to restrain her. Josephine fought to get loose; she kicked and pushed in an effort to get away. She kept screaming that she had to get to her aunt.

The policewoman hailed a medic from one of the ambulances that had arrived. "Give the child the strongest sedative you're allowed to administer, and get her to a hospital."

The medic went to get the sedatives from his ambulance but told the policewoman he was not allowed to take Josephine to a hospital. "Why not?" the officer asked.

"She isn't wounded," the medic replied.

"Yes, you can. You now have an order from a policewoman to do so. If you don't, I'll make sure you wish you had."

Just before a heavily restrained Josephine was placed in the ambulance, another officer ran up. "Hold on. You can't leave before she identifies the victim. I heard her say it's her aunt."

The officer who intercepted Josephine and still held her in a firm embrace trying to console her wanted none of that. "Don't you dare come any closer to this child. No way will I allow you to take her to see the victim. What kind of an imbecile are you?"

"Watch your language! I outrank you. I insist she identify the victim before I'll let her leave."

The female officer turned to the two medics who had helped her get Josephine into the ambulance. "Close the door and get this crate moving. Hurry, let's get out of here. I'll take care of this creep later." The ambulance left with the sirens on, leaving one very angry policeman behind.

At the hospital, they managed to calm Josephine down enough to get the telephone numbers of her father and her mother from her. An emergency room doctor who was experienced in making these types of calls was asked to call Caroline and Jason. Josephine also managed to give Jerry's number.

Jason and Jerry were in the Milbank factory in Syosset when they received the call. They raced out to the car to drive to Manhattan. Before they got to the car, Jason's secretary called after them to stop. "The two of you can't drive. It's too dangerous to drive in your condition. I've called Hawkins. He'll be right out. He'll drive you to the hospital. Don't worry! He knows the city!"

From the car, Jerry called Caroline. She was in Roslyn, where they had moved right after the wedding. Caroline had already gotten the call from the doctor and was about to leave for the hospital. "No! I don't want you driving." Jerry was very upset but his voice was still forceful. "Wait for us. Jason and I are in the car and we'll pick you up. Right now we're less than ten minutes from our house, and it's on the way to Manhattan. Sit tight; we'll be there any minute."

When the three of them arrived at the hospital they were taken directly to see the heavily sedated Josephine. The nurse who took them up to Josephine's room took one look at Caroline and called an intern to also give her some sedatives.

At that point, the three of them had no idea where Kristy was and if she was still alive. Jerry took the nurse aside and asked. The nurse had no idea but promised to check if the hospital had a report. Before the nurse returned with the information, a hospital administrator entered the room and signaled Jerry and Jason to step outside. Once outside the room, they received the bad news. Kristy was never taken to a hospital. She was pronounced dead at the scene and taken directly to the city morgue.

Jason had been holding up pretty well, but this was too much. He broke down, and Jerry did his best to console him. Between his tears, Jason asked if he could see Kristy. The administrator shook her head. "Not yet. The car was going pretty fast, and the impact caused severe damage. The good part is, she did not suffer. She was killed instantly, and was no longer with us when the car dragged her along and crashed into the coffee shop. Please go back into the room and I'll order some sedatives for you, too."

Jason refused to go back into the room. He was not ready to tell Josephine and Caroline that Kristy was dead. The hospital administrator suggested they take a moment in the small visitor's waiting room down the hall. Jerry volunteered to go and inform Caroline and Josephine, but Jason insisted that he should be the one to tell them about Kristy.

XXXIV

Kristy was buried in Huntington Rural Cemetery, a beautiful cemetery on Long Island six miles from the factory in Syosset. Services were held in the small chapel on the cemetery grounds. Noah arrived a day before the funeral. He was in his head office in Chicago when he received the news that Kristy had died. He immediately left for his apartment in The Streeter, a luxury apartment complex near Michigan Avenue and Lake Shore Drive. When he called to get his plane ready to take him to New York, he learned that the plane was being serviced. It would not be ready by the next day. He asked his chauffer how long it would take to drive. When he heard how long the drive would take he decided to wait and take the plane. He offered to pick up Kitty, who lived in Bayville. Bayville is located in McHenry County and is only forty miles from the loop. Noah planned to ask his chauffer to get her when his plane was ready to take them to New York.

When Noah called her, Kitty had already left for New York. The moment she got the news, she knew Jason would need her support. She left immediately to be by his side. When she arrived in New York, she realized Josephine and Caroline needed as much support as Jason and that she had to be the strong one.

A week after the funeral, Kitty closed the big house in Bayville and moved in with Jason in his Manhattan apartment. Now she was also close to Caroline and Josephine. Every day, she drove with Jason to the factory in Syosset, dropped him off, and took the car to Roslyn.

For a while there was talk that Josephine would need the help of a psychiatrist. She kept blaming herself for Kristy's death. As she told Caroline, "If only I'd been more careful, I would have seen that car coming."

Jason was very patient with her, trying to talk that idea out of her head. "No matter what you keep telling me, people can look only one way at a time. You were looking towards Times Square. I would have been doing the same thing. I have seen Times Square hundreds of times, and you were just visiting. It would have been very unusual for you to be looking the other way. Nobody is expected to be looking out for cars that jump the curb.

"You know I loved Kristy dearly and I miss her daily. She is the greatest hero I know; in her own way, she gave me you. Without her unbelievably unselfish heroism, I would have lost you. Just think of it; for Kristy to love you so much to be willing to offer her life for you, you must be a very special person. Now don't disappoint her! Don't sit around and waste your life obsessed with the foolish thought that somehow you are responsible for her death. That is nonsense, and you have no right detracting from her memory in any way, and certainly not by feeling guilty. Honor her by making the very best you can of the life she gave you. Of the life she wanted you to have because she loved you so much. Make your life a tribute to Kristy's memory."

Jason must have gotten through. Josephine threw her arms around his neck. "Dad, I promise. I'll make her proud of me. I'll show people what a wonderful person Kristy was." That she meant it was evident by her school grades. After the accident, her grades had dropped from B-plusses or better to D's and failing. After Jason's talk they went right back up and for the remainder of the school year she had mainly A's.

She kept it up. And in her junior year her grades were so good that when she applied to Stanford at the beginning of her senior year, she was accepted. It was not clear how much it helped that she was on the varsity field hockey team for three years and had won numerous medals in skiing.

After Josephine left for college, life more or less returned to normal for the others. Kitty moved back to Bayville, and Jason returned to traveling the way he did before he had married Kristy.

XXXV

L ife at Stanford was not an immediate success for Josephine. The first disappointment came when she learned that, like all freshmen, she was not allowed to bring her car. She had never relied on public transportation, and now she had to take the Marguerite Shuttle if she wanted to go into town. Then there was the selection of her roommates. She was assigned to a suite in one of the residence halls with three other girls. The person who made the selection of the girls to share the four-person suite must have had some kind of class war in mind. Mandy Jackson, a black girl, was from Detroit. Both her parents were doctors. Her father was a well-known orthopedic surgeon and her mother was head of the optometry department at the university hospital. Morgan Leland was from Branchville, Alabama. Both her parents worked for Superior Manufacturing, the local clothing factory. Barbara Hamell was from Columbia, South Carolina. Her father drove a city bus. The latter two girls were on full scholarship, and, of course, Mandy and Josephine were not.

During the very first week, hateful remarks started. Josephine overheard Morgan say to Barbara, "Those rich bitches think they are something special."

When Josephine complained about it to Mandy, Mandy laughed it off. "I'd rather be called a rich bitch than nigger. That term has been floating around here too."

The atmosphere in the suite remained tense for the better part of the first semester. It didn't help matters that Josephine found out that keeping up with her bright classmates was quite different from getting A's at P. J. Richard Memorial. She almost decided to quit and go home. What stopped her was what she promised her father; she was not going to disappoint Kristy.

One evening, Josephine called a meeting of the suite mates. Reluctantly, Morgan and Barbara attended. Josephine had decided to be blunt, and she was. Looking at Morgan and Barbara she said, "The two of you think of Mandy and me as rich bitches. Rich, yes, but I don't think we are bitches. If you call us that, then *you* are the bitches. Both of us are proud our families have become rich.

"Mandy's parents worked hard to become doctors. They bucked all odds to become as successful as they are. At one time they too were scholarship students, like you two. But, unlike you, they had to overcome racial prejudice and people trying to hold them back because of it. Even today some people think Mandy is here because of affirmative action. You know damn well that is not true. She is probably the most brilliant student in our entire class. She has helped me pass many difficult exams, and if you reach out to her, she will do the same for you."

Josephina wasn't finished. "My father and his father are also brilliant. I only wish I had their brains. They have used their talents to create things, most of all, plenty of jobs. Neither of them has ever done anything dishonest or cheated others. On the contrary. It is a fact that, in their companies, discrimination is not tolerated, and they pay all their employees very well. Like Mandy, I too am proud of my family.

"I have never met your folks but I'm proud of them, too. The two of you are here heading for a better life than your parents have. That is not just because you are here on scholarship. Your parents put you in a position to earn that scholarship. That is very hard. Many parents of kids you went to school with failed, and their kids are heading nowhere. You were lucky to have great parents."

Josephine paused for a moment and looked at the three others. "Now, let's stop bitching at each other. Let's take full advantage of all that is given to us and do our very best to earn it."

The room was silent until Barbara got up. She spoke directly to Mandy. "I'm so ashamed I used the word *nigger*. My father would kill me if he knew. His supervisor is black, and Dad swears by the man. As a young man, my dad made some serious mistakes, and if it wasn't for his supervisor he would still be paying for those youthful indiscretions."

Mandy was a good sport about it. "Don't lose sleep over it, Barbara. We all use words and expressions without thinking they might hurt someone. The worst I ever did was using the expression 'I jewed him down' when describing the purchase I made in a small dress shop. My friend from West Bloomfield, a suburb of Detroit where we lived, got very angry. It was only then that I realized what the expression really meant."

Not to be outdone, Josephine jumped right in. "Tell me about it. I was visiting my late aunt in New York City, telling her about an incident at my school. I said 'He japped me out.' Boy, did I get an earful from her!"

Morgan had been silent while the others enthusiastically swapped these "slips" on their part. "Let me start by saying I'm in. I'm all for ending this feud that has been dividing this suite into two camps. I've always been at the bottom of the pile, and once I got here at Stanford, I enjoyed kicking back a little. But one thing you said, Josephine, got my attention. You said your dad and his father always paid their employees well. That has not been part of my world. Both my mom and dad never received even minimum wage, and their employer cheated on overtime. It was hard knowing how hard they worked to be able to afford the things my brother and I needed. Rather than buying things they needed, they saved every penny they could to buy a computer so my brother and I did not have to go to the library to do our homework.

"I adore my mom and dad, and really hated the rich people who exploited them. I knew it was a generalization, but I couldn't help it. Listening to the three of you makes things different. Here are three classy girls saying they want to be my friends. That has never happened to me before. I've always been white trash from Branchville, Alabama. Unless you have been in my position, you have no idea what it means to be sitting in a dorm at Stanford talking to my roommates who accept me as an equal. Sounds corny, but I would like to get up and hug you guys."

Spontaneously, they all got up and in the middle of the room they hugged and laughed; they were celebrating that the feud was over. That marked the beginning of what became known on campus as the Four Musketeers.

At the end of their sophomore year, the girls feared their foursome would be broken up. For some reason that was not fully explained to her, Morgan was informed her scholarship could not be continued for her junior year. Without her full scholarship, there was no way she could return for the next school year.

Around this time, Noah Housten came to visit his granddaughter. Business had brought him to San Francisco, and it was his habit that whenever he was in the neighborhood, he would drop in to see Josephine. Unannounced, he knocked on the door of Josephine's suite. As usual, she was ecstatic to see him, but when he entered the room he noticed the girls were not their usual happy selves.

"What's going on, ladies? The four of you seem worried." Josephine explained that Morgan would not be returning for her junior year. Noah was surprised. "Why not come back, Morgan? I thought you liked it here."

"I do. I like it a lot, but I won't have a scholarship. Without that support, there is no way I can afford to come back. My folks don't have that kind of money."

It did not take Noah long to think of a solution. "Why don't you apply for the Kristy Housten Memorial Scholarship? Jo Jo should have told you about it."

Josephine was confused. "Never heard of it. Is there really such a thing?"

"Sure is. Morgan, give me your full name and home address and I'll see to it you get the application forms."

Eagerly, Morgan wrote the information on a piece of paper and handed it to Noah. Noah took it and wrote on it "The Kristy Housten full two-year scholarship is awarded to Morgan Leland." None of the girls could see what he wrote down and when he handed it to Morgan she let out a scream. "Really? Really? Is this for real?"

"Sure is," Noah replied with a satisfied smile on his face.

When Morgan showed the paper to the others, Noah got attacked by all four of them. He had been hugged and kissed before, but never by four twenty-year-olds at the same time. Josephine looked at him with tears in her eyes. She had never been more proud of her granpa.

Morgan could not thank him enough but Noah shrugged it off. "I'm the one who should be grateful. Morgan, great young women like you make it all worthwhile. Having a nice company and flying around in a private plane only goes so far. What makes everything really worthwhile is the privilege of helping others. What good is having money if you can't use it to correct a situation that is not right? I don't know why your scholarship was not continued, and I don't really care. It is a blessing for me to help a wonderful young lady like you finish her education. Morgan, I want you to contact me if you want to continue on after undergraduate school. I'll feel hurt if you don't. The same counts for you, Barbara. The four of you have been close friends, and all four deserve the same chance to receive the education you want."

Mandy could not resist giving Noah another hug. "Josephine, you really know your grandfather. What you told me about him was no exaggeration. It's all true. You never brag about him but I will tell people about my good friend's grandfather, or Granpa, as she calls him."

XXXVI

J ason found living alone in his big Manhattan apartment unbearable. His traveling increased to an extent that he hardly visited the factory in Syosset, and even missed a few company board meetings. During his absence his partner, Jerry Collins, became the acting CEO as well as subbing as chairman of the board.

Due to Jason's efforts, Milbank's foreign business was booming, and much of the company's profits came from their overseas sales. Rather than return these profits to the States, the board decided to keep the money abroad. Over time, this became a huge amount.

At about the same time, the board considered a plan the build a factory in Ireland and transfer much of the production from Syosset to the proposed plant. Jason caught wind of this plan when he heard Milbank had made a bid on a substantial piece of property in Ireland. He returned to the United States and called a board meeting. In the meeting, he announced his opposition to the plan. He made it very clear that Jerry and he had enough shares to oust any board member who favored the plan. He also instructed Milbank's outside accounting firm to start a process by which the company could bring most of the money held in foreign countries back to the States.

Jason was caught off guard when two of Milbank's board members resigned and joined Horizon Investment, a company that made a hostile bid to take over Milbank. Jason thought he and Jerry controlled enough shares to stave off the bid. He was wrong. Horizon made a bid for all outstanding shares. Their bid offered a premium of $20 above the market value of the shares. The response was big, and many of what Jason thought were "safe" shares got into the hands of Horizon. In an effort to stem the tide, Jason started buying shares. He had few liquid assets and was too proud to ask his father for help, so he mortgaged his apartment to get the funds he needed.

Horizon forced a company meeting. They said they had enough shares and proxy ballots to elect a new board and oust Jason and Jerry. Jason was confident this was not going to happen. According to his count, Jerry and he controlled enough shares to win by a comfortable margin.

Jason was stunned when in the meeting, Jerry used his shares and the proxies he held to support Horizon. Horizon immediately installed a new board of directors. The new board ousted Jason as chairman and CEO. Without speaking to any-one, Jason left the ballroom where the meeting was being held and disappeared into nowhere. For ten days, no one knew where he was. Some even feared he might have done something drastic, like take his own life.

After ten days, Jason appeared at the factory to claim his personal possessions from his office. Julie, his long-time secretary, told him the board had appointed Jerry as the new CEO and Joe Humphrey, one of the men who quit the original board to join Horizon, had been elected chairman. Julie said she had handed in her resignation and was leaving at the end of the month. Julie was getting along in age and Jason worried where she could go.

"I'm not staying here!" Julie was adamant. "No way will I work for these bastards. I know damn well when they move operations to Ireland they'll fire most of the folks here with just a pittance for a sev-erance package. Jason, some of these people have worked here for more than a decade. How can they do that?"

Jason had no answer. Julie knew him well enough to know he was not worried about his own future as much as he was worried about that of his former employees.

Jason was packing some of his mementos from early trips abroad when Jerry appeared at the door to his office. Jason looked up. His first impulse was to throw the heavy bronze statue of *Manneken Pis* at Jerry.

He controlled his anger and said, "Et tu, Brute?" He pointed at the door in a gesture for Jerry to get the hell out. Jerry took the hint and disappeared into the hall.

When Jason left the building, most of the office and factory staff poured into the parking lot. They formed a path all the way to his car. There were so many people that both sides of the path were three to four deep with employees tying to pay tribute to the man they loved. Some had tears in their eyes. The most touching moment was when Frankie, one of Jason's first employees, ran to the car to open the door for Jason. As Jason got in, Frankie raised his hand in a salute. He could not control himself; he reached in through the driver's-side window and hugged Jason.

Just outside the company gate, Jason was stopped by the big, black company limousine. Hawkins got out and signaled for Jason to get out of his car and get into the back of the limousine. Jason protested. "Hawkins, what are you doing?"

Hawkins was wearing his full uniform. "I'm driving you home, sir. No matter what happened you are still my hero, sir. Freddy will follow us and put your car in the garage in your building." This was the first time Jason had sat in back of the limousine while Hawkins drove.

On the way into Manhattan, Hawkins told Jason that Jerry made him drive him home in the limousine every evening. He was also required to pick up Jerry at his home in Roslyn at eight o'clock every morning.

When Hawkins pulled up to Jason's apartment building, he quickly got out of the car and opened the door for Jason. Like Frankie, he saluted Jason as he said, "Good-bye, Boss. It has been a privilege working for you."

XXXVII

J ason was sitting in one of the big leather chairs in front of the window overlooking the park. He had been sitting there quietly for several hours, thinking things over. The farewell he had received that morning at the factory had deeply moved him, and he felt he had let his employees down. He should have done a better job looking out for them but the question was, how?

He heard a knock on the door. The doorman had not announced a visitor so it had to be someone from the building. When he opened the door he was surprised to see Caroline standing in front of him. "Hey, stop staring. May I come in?"

"Sorry, you surprised me. Of course, come on in."

"I'm not staying with that bastard! I hit him with a saucepan when I found out what he did. I walked out and I've been staying at a hotel. He has no idea where I am."

Jason was still staring at her. "You what? Where?"

"I said I hit that bastard. I'm never going back to Jerry. That fucking traitor! How could he? I always suspected he was jealous of you, but this . . ."

Jason recovered enough to get Caroline to sit down and tell him in a more coherent way what she had done. Caroline, still highly emotional, sat down. "First, give me some of that Scotch you have been drinking."

Jason went to get Caroline a glass and poured her a hefty shot from the bottle that was sitting next to his chair. He sat down opposite her and said, "Hi, Caroline, nice to see you. Just in time; I needed someone to talk to."

That loosened Caroline up. "Sorry, I was so excited and wound up . . . but I'm so mad I could not help it. Yes, I also need someone to talk to."

"Who goes first?" Jason asked.

"Me, of course," Caroline said jokingly, but she meant it.

"I knew about the bid to take over the company but I never had a clue Jerry supported the other side. Now I know they were planning all along to oust you, because you wanted to bring the money back home and opposed moving all those jobs to Ireland. While you were traveling, drumming up all that business, you trusted Jerry completely. I can't believe how he betrayed you. And the asshole didn't even realize I would hate him for it!"

Jason interrupted her. "Why would he? You're his wife. Why are you on my side?"

"Now you're making me angry. Of course I'm on your side. In the first place, what he did is dishonest.

He cheated. There is no way around that. Then, in case you forgot, you're the father of my child; and maybe, Mister Wise Guy, I like you better than him." Caroline stopped abruptly. She was shocked she had said the last part.

She was not the only one surprised by that admission. "But you married him. Didn't you love him?"

"Yes, I did. But that is different. Sure I loved Jerry, or I would not have married him and lived with him all these years. But after all these years, you still get under my skin. Okay, I have special feelings for you. Always have. Now I've said it! I wish you had not pulled that out of me."

After all the emotions of the morning, he did not think he could get shaken up even more but this made his head spin. As he took a long swallow from his drink, he carefully looked at Caroline. Memories of high school flooded his brain. *Her face is thinner and more mature than that of the girl I remember. She has gone from cute to pretty. I can't help staring at her. No, she is beautiful.*

Jason snapped out of it. "Okay, so you hit him with a saucepan and then what happened?"

"I screamed and yelled at him that what he had done was despicable. I told him I was leaving him. I went upstairs to pack a suitcase and he followed me, begging me not to leave. He tried to explain his side of the story but I would not listen. He tried to stop me from leaving the house. But I threatened to call the police, and he let me go.

"The next morning he had my car traced and came to the hotel I had checked into to ask me to come back. I threw him out of my room and when he left I grabbed my suitcase and fled to another hotel. This time I took a taxi and abandoned my car at the hotel so he could not trace my steps. He has no idea where I am.

"I tried to contact you, but no one knew where you were. Not until today, when Julie called my cell phone, did I know you were back. And just like a long time ago I've come crying on your doorstep."

"That's not correct. This time it is I who was attacked. Like a complete fool, I never saw it coming. I've been sitting here thinking things over. It was pure negligence on my part not to keep an eye on things. I was an absentee CEO. I paid for it, but what is much worse, all the employees are paying for my neglect."

Caroline moved a little closer. "Jason, stop it! I know you feel sorry for yourself and you have every right to do so. But it is pure nonsense to think that any of it is your fault. While you were out drumming up an amazing amount of sales, you left Jerry in charge. Was it negligent to trust him? No, it was not!

"The two of you founded the company together. He was your partner and friend. I'm sure you thought the company was as much his as yours. That's the stupid argument he gave me. He said he had all the right to do what he did because the company was just as much his, but you ran it like it was yours alone. I told him he was full of it. If that was true, why would you let him run the place while you concentrated on sales? And if he had different objectives from yours, why did he not have the decency to discuss that with you? Instead he hid everything from you and made agreements behind your back. I told him his objectives were less than honorable if not outright immoral. If you were wrong in trusting that slime-ball, what about me? I married him!"

The two of them got some comfort in repeatedly telling each other how bad a person Jerry was and that it was reasonable not to have seen it. After a couple more drinks they fell into reminiscing about their high school days. They even brought back the memory of Jason being accused of rape in South Korea.

Caroline asked, "Do you agree with the way your father has gone all out for Lilly?"

"Yes, I do. Don't forget, I agreed to partner with him in an attempt to buy that factory and then put Lilly in charge. Turns out she actually loved that guy Shin-Il Bai. She tried to protect him by going along with the plot. I don't think she had any idea how serious it would be if North Korea got their hands on one of our UT-500 computers. But I must say, buying an entire hotel just to give her and her husband a job is a little extreme. Ironically, it's been a huge financial success. Dad has had a return on his investment that is way above anything else he has invested in. Lilly and Il Bai turned out to be excellent hotel managers. They have returned his loyalty by turning down numerous offers to run much larger properties."

While they talked it got late, and at one point Caroline looked at her watch and realized it was time to return to her hotel. When saying good night, she wondered if she should kiss Jason. After a little hesitation, she decided a peck on the forehead would be okay.

At two in the morning Jason's phone rang. It was Caroline. "Can I come over? I dreamt Jerry tracked me down and physically dragged me to his car to take me home. In my dream he hit me several times and I woke up. I tried but I can't go back to sleep. I'm scared. Will it be okay if I come to your place? I'll feel much safer there."

"No problem, come on over. I've got plenty of room."

"You're sure now?"

"Of course. I'll tell the night porter I'm expecting you, so you can come right on up. By the way, how did you get in this afternoon without the doorman announcing you?"

"Oh, that was simple. The man thinks I'm your sister. He's seen me many times with Kristy and Josephine, so he's sure we are family."

When Jason hung up, he wondered if he should get dressed. He was only wearing pajama pants and did not feel that was right. Once he put on a shirt he thought he might as well put on a pair of regular pants also. When Caroline arrived she misinterpreted why he was fully dressed. "So you had trouble sleeping too. Did you even go to bed?"

Jason did not want to admit he got dressed because she was coming over. "I was catching up on all the magazines that piled up while I was traveling, and I fell asleep in my chair. I see you brought your suitcase. Did you check out of the hotel?"

Caroline blushed and she hoped Jason did not notice. "Yes, I think it is best if I keep moving around to eliminate the chance Jerry eventually catches up to me."

Jason bought her explanation. "That dream must have really gotten to you. Here, give me that suitcase. I'll put it in the guestroom for you. Want a drink before we turn in?"

"No thanks. I've had enough liquor for one day."

They said good night and disappeared into their separate rooms. Jason had barely changed back into pajamas when Caroline opened his bedroom door. "Damn it! I won't let it happen again. This time I am not sleeping in that room. I'm coming in here with you."

Jason did not know what to say. He wanted what was happening but he was not sure how to handle it. Maybe she was just looking for the security of being near him. That dream must have really scared her, but . . . Caroline was wearing a robe and he was sure she was not wearing her street clothes underneath. She wanted more than just being near him for security.

"We're adults now, Jason. I'm sure you no longer worry about what Mom would think about this."

"I always thought you could never forgive me for the way I acted when you came to tell me you were expecting. I know we have become very good friends since. But I thought something might have lingered."

"Jason, that was ages ago. So much has happened since. Besides, eventually I understood; you were just not ready for the commitment of a marriage. As far as that goes, I could feel that you are still hurt I withheld Josephine from you for many years. Don't you think it's time to forget and live in the present?"

"We do have a beautiful child, don't we?" As Jason said it, he went over to Caroline. "Does the mother of that beautiful child mind if the father of that beautiful child kisses that child's beautiful mother?"

"Do I have to wait much longer while you make beautiful speeches?"

Their kiss lasted forever. Finally Caroline asked, "Can we make this a little more romantic?" She went over and dimmed the lights. She removed her robe and carefully took off the negligee she was wearing underneath. She pointed at Jason. "Your turn."

After Jason had taken off his pajamas, he took Caroline by the hand and led her to the bed. Playfully she pushed him onto the bed and jumped on top of him. While pressing her naked body to his she whispered in his ear, "This is a starry-eyed high school girl's dream come true."

XXXVIII

Jason awoke from something pushing against him. It was Caroline readjusting herself. She was tightly snuggled up against him, and he could feel her hair on his chest as she tightened her arms around him. She was fast asleep, and he dared not move, afraid to wake her.

For a long time he lay quietly thinking about their days together in high school. Then his thoughts turned to Kristy. He made an effort not to mix his thoughts together. He did not want to compare the two women. Certainly not after making love to Caroline for most of the night. He was afraid that thinking about them in the same thought would come down to sex, and that would cheapen the way he felt about both Caroline and Kristy.

As if she read his thoughts, Caroline woke up. She sat up and stretched. The sheet fell away from her shoulders and Jason looked at her well preserved breasts. He could not help thinking, *those have not changed much since high school.*

Caroline noticed what he was looking at but ignored it. "Wow, I slept like a baby. How did you sleep?" Without waiting for his answer she continued. "That was great last night. I love you Jason, I always have." She pulled the sheet up around her shoulder and continued in a much more serious tone. "Sorry, but I have to ask. Will I always have to compete with Kristy's memory?"

Jason did not like the question one bit. He was still struggling with that very question and did not know the answer. "Did you feel that way last night?"

"No, that's why I ask. When we made love it felt like you loved me a lot. It felt like the two of us reconnected. The way we felt about each other back in high school. For lack of a better word, it had that sincerity."

Jason got up and put on his robe. "I can honestly say that Kristy was not there last night. Her memory did not come between us, and I don't know if I should feel guilty about that. Was I untrue to her? I just don't know. Put on your robe and let's go make some coffee in the kitchen and discuss this."

"I'm glad you are willing to discuss this. It will influence our relationship and our future together . . . if there is one."

After they both had a cup of coffee and grabbed a box of horribly stale donuts from the refrigerator, they down at the kitchen table. The table was a beautiful antique mahogany table Kristy had bought at an auction. Jason went to get some coasters, which he carefully placed beneath their hot cups. The significance of that did not escape Caroline. She knew how proud Kristy had been of the table. She never failed to tell visitors how she had discovered the table at an auction and won the bid because everybody failed to look up its origin.

Jason started their discussion. "In case you have any doubts, I want you to stay with me. I feel like we have rediscovered each other. I love you. Please stay."

"You did not hear my silent prayer but as we sat down I prayed you would say you wanted me back in your life. I know what Kristy meant to you but I love you enough to live with your memory of her."

"As you say that, my feelings for you keep growing. Part of me feels guilty and stupid for not marrying you way back when we were still going together. But I'm conflicted. I loved Kristy so much that I can't imagine not having had those wonderful years with her."

"I agree with the wonderful years with Kristy. She was great! I loved her. She was probably the best friend I ever had. I too miss her a lot. I don't agree with you feeling guilty and stupid. If we had married at that point in our lives, we'd probably be divorced and bitter now. You were not ready, and certainly not capable of substituting me for the company. I would have been a distant second, vying constantly for your attention. That's why I never told you I was pregnant. I could not have lived a life competing with your company."

Jason looked at her admiringly. "You make it sound so clean. So natural. You're making Kristy sound like *our* memory, one we can share."

"That's the way it should be. Without her, we could not have this conversation. She is the one who managed to divorce your persona from your company. She made it possible that there was a Jason and there was his company and the two were not fused into one. I'll be forever grateful to her for that. And I'm grateful I forced myself on you that day in the motel. It gave us Josephine."

"You're something else! That's why I fell head over heels for you in high school. I've been thinking about that. Those were fabulous years for us. They could never have been that great for me if it weren't for an immensely popular athlete who fell in love with a brainy nerd."

Caroline stood up and was about to sit on Jason's lap when the phone rang.

"Jason, thank God you're home. I've been calling every day trying to find you. Are you all right?"

"Yes, Mom. Still a little shaken about what happened at the company meeting but I'm fine. Other good things are happening."

"What does that mean?"

"Here, I'll let you hear for yourself." With that Jason handed the phone to Caroline.

"Hi, Mom. Yes, he's doing fine. Actually, *we're* doing fine."

"Oh, good. I'm happy you're with him. I was worried sick the last few days. He wasn't home. Did you just get there?"

"No, I got here last night. I hope you are not mad, but I committed adultery."

For a while it was silent on the other end of the phone and Caroline said, "Mom? Mom, are you still there?"

"Yes, dear, I'm still here. I needed a moment to realize what you said. I'm just bursting with joy. My kids are finally together. It has taken so long, but my son and daughter are finally back together."

"Mom, that sounds bad. I can't go to bed with my brother."

"You're right! I'm sorry, but I can't help thinking of you as my daughter. But I'm so happy; I've so wanted the two of you to get back together. What about Jerry? He's your husband; doesn't that complicate things?"

"After what he did to Jason, I don't consider him my husband anymore. I want that bastard out of my life."

"Amen to that. We all feel that way; unbelievable what he did. But I can't say I really hate him. My kids are back together and he helped."

Kitty stayed on the phone for a long time. She was not prying, but wanted to hear that Caroline had moved in and would stay with Jason from now on, even though she was not yet divorced from Jerry.

Jason asked his mother not to say anything to anybody until he had to chance to tell them about Caroline and him. Next he wanted to call Noah.

Jason looked at the big kitchen clock. "I don't want to call him on his cell. I have no idea where he is today and I shouldn't tell him our news while he is traveling. I'll see if he's in his office after we get dressed."

Caroline had another idea. "Can't it wait for a moment longer? I was hoping we could take a shower together. Remember as kids we talked about it? But we never had a chance to do it. Mom would have killed us if she caught us. Now, she would think it's a great idea. Growing a little older isn't all bad."

Jason agreed; it was a great idea.

In the shower Caroline made a mistake. While the water was shooting at them from all sides she asked, "Did Kristy and you ever shower together in this crazy shower?"

Jason did not like it. "We're not going to go there, remember? Just pass me the soap and I'll do your back."

"Sorry, I didn't mean anything by it other than express my amazement at this huge shower with water spraying from all sides."

Later that day, Jason did reach his dad at his office. Noah was less surprised than Kitty, but certainly not less happy to hear about Jason and Caroline getting together. He wanted to know why Jason did not ask him for help in fighting the takeover of Milbank.

"Dad, I never saw it coming. I was convinced Jerry and I would defeat Horizon's attempt at a take-over. Jerry never gave me a clue as to what he was planning."

"He fooled all of us. I always thought the two of you made a great team, and often thought I would have liked a partner like that to help run my company. On the other hand, our stay in South Korea convinced me that Caroline was still in love with you."

"It did? Or are you saying that to make me feel good?"

"No, Jason, I'm not making it up. I asked Caroline to come along with me to South Korea because of her concern for you when I told Kitty and her that you had been arrested. Not for a moment did she believe you were guilty. She and Kristy became friends on the plane even before we landed in Korea but the way Caroline looked at you when you were finally released made me suspect she still carried a torch for you.

"Now, on a completely different subject, do you want me to help you get Milbank back? Money won't be a problem."

"Thanks, Dad. I really appreciate the offer. To be truthful, I'm tearing up because my father offered to do that for me. But Horizon and Jerry own too much stock. Besides, they have adopted the so-called 'poison pill' as a strategy to defend against hostile takeovers."

"Okay. Let me say then how delighted I am at this turn of events. Remember, if the two of you want to get away for a while, the chalet and the Korean hotel are at your disposal."

Caroline, who had been listening in on the other phone, shouted, "Yes! I want to go to both places with Jason. Noah, I love you! After all these years can I call you Dad? May I, please? Pretty soon I hope to be your daughter-in-law, but I want you to be my dad, Dad. You know, like my father, the way Kitty has been my mom."

Noah was touched. "Now who's tearing up? Caroline, like Kitty, I too adore you. I love that stubborn son of mine, but the truth is, I've always been on your side. How could I not love you? You gave me Jo Jo."

It was time to end the mutual admiration society. Caroline and Jason had to discuss how to tell Josephine.

Caroline did not want to tell her by phone. She wanted to be able to hold her daughter in her arms when she told her how much she loved her father. Jason agreed, and he invited Josephine to come to New York so he could explain to her how he lost the factory. Kitty had told them Josephine had read about it in the newspaper and called her because she could not contact her father. So it would be normal for him to call and tell her he was okay, and that he would like to tell her what happened. Josephine was eager to come and see her father and agreed to fly to New York the next weekend.

When Jason opened his apartment door, Josephine saw Caroline standing behind him. She froze for a moment, staring at Caroline. Then she flew around her mother's neck. It was hard to tell if she was crying or laughing.

She was shouting, "You're together! Mom and Dad are together! Oh my God, Mommy, you're with Dad! Please tell me it's forever. Oh, this is so great!"

Next she embraced Jason. "Daddy, it's true, isn't it? Mommy and you are living here in your apartment."

Caroline was amazed. "How on earth did you know?"

"You're not wearing that 'going out' makeup you always put on before you leave the house. You wouldn't have come here without it. So I knew immediately that you live here now. I saw you standing there and your beautiful face is aglow. No makeup; you look so happy. Come here, I want to hug both of you at the same time."

When she had both her parents encircled in her arms, she said, "I can finally say it. I hate Jerry. Always have, but I could never say it. I had to pretend to like him."

Jason asked her, "You hate him for what he did to me?"

"No, I hated him from the beginning. Way back when he came to see Mom. You all thought I was jealous, but I couldn't stand the man. I'm not the least bit surprised what he did to you, Daddy. The man is a creep. He even has those shady-looking eyes. Oh, Mom, I'm so happy you're here with Dad and no longer with that man!"

XXXIX

It took Jerry ten days to discover that Caroline was staying with Jason. He called, trying to talk to her. Jason answered the phone. Caroline could hear Jerry demand loudly, "Let me speak to Caroline!"

Jason remained icy-calm. "Can't say I'm happy to hear from you, so let's make this short. You have my company, and I have your wife. I win! Good-bye." With that, Jason hung up.

For the next half-hour the phone rang constantly, but Jason did not pick up. Finally Jerry left a voice mail message and stopped calling. They could hear the message as he was recording it. "You think you're so damn smart, don't you! Always playing the boss. Jason the genius, the great entrepreneur. Did you forget that without the money I brought in you would never have gotten started? I helped build the factory; you never gave me credit for that. I'll sue you for alienation of affection, you bastard!"

Jason looked at Caroline. "Is he right? Did I push him aside?"

Caroline assured Jason that Jerry had no cause to feel that way. "I can't imagine what he is thinking other than the fact that he is mad as hell. I left him. He is more than just mad. The man is hurt. I know he loves me, and I have to admit that he was a good husband. My friends always teased me that he treated me like a princess. But what he did to you is really unforgivable. For God's sake, he had full control of the factory while you were traveling all over the world trying to forget your sorrow. To tell you the truth, I never understood why you needed his approval of the sales contracts you negotiated before they went into production."

"That was the arrangement. Like when he voted my stock if I could not attend a meeting. I always thought of him as my partner. He was my best friend. Actually, there were times when he was my only friend. I never pushed him aside!"

"Calm down. You don't have to feel guilty. We'll never know what spooks got into his head. I suspect it was just plain greed and an ego he could not control. If *you* misjudged him, what about me? I refuse to accept he was always that way. Josephine saw something we missed. We should go see a lawyer; I want a divorce as soon as possible."

The next day, the two of them went to see Henry Woodland at Woodland, Kagan, Cummings, and Williams. That was the law firm Milbank frequently used. When Caroline told Henry she had come to see him because she wanted to divorce Jerry, he explained he could not represent her because Jerry had already engaged one of his partners. He referred her to Cesar Cavallo, a one-man law firm specializing in divorce.

Cesar told Caroline she might have a case on grounds of cruel and inhuman treatment that made it impossible for her to continue to reside with Jerry as husband and wife. He cautioned her that Jerry's participation in the hostile takeover of Milbank must have caused such mental anguish that it endangered her health. "That's going to be a tough one. My suggestion is to let him go ahead and sue you on grounds of adultery. You seem comfortable with admitting to it, so why not let him sue on those grounds. You tell me both of you signed pre-nups so there will be little or no problem reaching a property settlement. Your daughter is over eighteen, and anyway, she is not his. So no problem there either."

Caroline was surprised. "So I can just sit back and do nothing and let him divorce me?"

"That's all there is to it, unless you want to help him and send him a signed affidavit admitting adultery. Just kidding. I know Benny Williams very well. I'll contact him and propose we settle this matter quickly. I don't think Jason has much to worry about either. Jerry's threat to sue for alienation of affection does not amount to much. I'm sure Benny will tell him that and advise him to just settle for a speedy divorce."

XL

Sherry Segelman called. Caroline was happy to hear from her. "Hey, Sherry. Great you called. How did you get this number?" Sherry was president of the Lady Volunteers. Lady Volunteers was a group of women who sponsored various activities around town, mostly for the benefit of the less fortunate. Membership was by invitation only. Although there were no published criteria for membership, you had to have enough money to keep up with the donations required to sponsor the activities. Caroline considered the group worthwhile; she was a past president.

Sherry's answer was curt. "Never mind how I got your number. Rumors are flying around Roslyn that you have left Jerry and are now in an adulterous relationship with his former partner."

"Whoa, let me explain."

"I do not need your explanation, Caroline. Adultery is unacceptable in our circles. Jerry deserves better than a slut for a wife. The members of Lady Volunteers have instructed me to tell you they no longer want you around. You are officially expelled; good-bye." She hung up.

Caroline was stunned. She ran into the office part of the apartment where Jason was talking with Jeffrey Milkowsky. Ignoring Jeffrey, she ran to Jason. She fell over her own words, "Jason! Sherry Segelman just called me a slut!"

Jason had no idea who Sherry Segelman was. He asked Caroline to explain. "She is president this year of Lady Volunteers back in Roslyn. They do a lot of very good work, and I've been president. Now she said they consider me a slut because I left Jerry and am living with you!"

"Fine group of friends you had."

"Jason, this is serious. Jerry is smearing my reputation. I can't just let that happen!"

"I hear you, baby. But what can we do? Can you go back there and explain what happed?"

"She can't. But I can." It was Jeffrey who spoke up.

"If you don't mind me butting in, I can take care of this."

Caroline had no idea who Jeffrey was and how in the world he could help her.

Jason hastily introduced Jerry. "Jeffrey has worked with me from the very beginning. Together we developed Milbank's very first products. He is a true electronic genius and the brains behind those first products."

Jeffrey shook his head. "Jason is being modest. We dreamed up those products together. I got myself fired from the original Milbank owned by Mr. Housten, Jason's father. When nobody would hire me, it was Jason who offered me a job and brought me back into the company. I have worked for him ever since. Until two weeks ago I was head of production at Milbank. I just dropped by to tell Jason I resigned. There is no way I'll work for those bastards.

"Jerry is stupid enough to think I will go to Ireland to help set up their new factory. No way! Production of the UT-500 will stay in the United States, but they say they don't need me for further development of that computer. A crop of new developers will be put in charge of that. Good luck with that! Jason and I developed that machine, and we know the ins and outs of that model better than anybody!"

Caroline started feeling better. *Maybe this guy can actually do something for me. He called Jerry stupid, and boy, does he sound angry.*

Jeffrey explained what he could do. "My wife is good friends with a reporter for one of the regional papers on Long Island. Her name is Hana Shepley. The paper covers most of Long Island. They have a big circulation, and I have heard from Hana that they have a lot of subscribers in Roslyn, where you lived.

"I'm sure Hana will give me an interview. I'll tell her why I left the company. I'll explain that they will move much of the production to Ireland and hundreds of people on Long Island will lose their jobs. I'll give her all the details. How moving production to Ireland was Jerry's plan, and how Jason fought it and that's how he lost control of the factory he built. Jason has just told me you and he have been friends since high school. I'll throw that in for good measure."

Hana Shepley did much more than interview Jeffrey. She did some careful research and visited the factory several times. To gain entry to the factory, she talked a safety inspector into letting her come along on his inspections. During these visits, she interviewed a lot of disgruntled employees; among them were both Frankie and Hawkins. She even managed to dig up the telephone number of Julie, Jason's former secretary.

When Hana presented her completed story to her editor, he decided to put it on the front page. Under the headline "Milbank Moving to Ireland" was the full story, including a stock photo of Jason and Jerry introducing a new computer at an international trade show. The story had a quote from Julie in which she gave a glowing account of Jason, her former boss. Jerry did not fare so well. Hana went out on a limb. Her editor did not cut the part in which she wrote that the shock of so many people losing their jobs was too much for Jerry's wife, and that she had since left Roslyn to live with childhood friends.

Jerry tried to sue the paper, but because everything in the story was factual, he did not stand a chance of succeeding. His lawyer advised him to lay low and ignore the story altogether. According to his lawyer, he would make matters worse by keeping it in the news. Jerry refused to take that advice and sued anyway. The judge looked at all the evidence and dismissed the suit. As his lawyer had advised him, the suit only brought attention once more to the story. Some people who had never read it looked up the online edition of the paper and read the story.

XLI

Once Jason and Jeffrey got together again, they fell into their old habit of dreaming up new, advanced products. To develop these products, they needed a factory, or at a minimum, a fully staffed research department. That would require a massive amount of money. Both Jason and Caroline had access to funds, but those funds were not nearly enough to get the project started. Among others, Jason approached his father.

His father looked carefully at their plans, but turned them down. Jason explained to his father that they only needed enough to get started. "We're by no means asking you to fund a large part. All we need is some more seed money so we can go ahead and approach some venture capital firms."

Noah explained why he did not believe in the project. "Jason, it looks to me too much like you two are out for revenge. You think you can get back at the folks who took over Milbank by building a more advanced version of the famous UT-500. Revenge is a bad driving force. It leads you to develop an unrealistic business plan. I've looked at your plans. They are based on developing advanced computers. That in itself is fine. But your plans call for these computers to be based on the technology used in the production of the UT-500, the same technology the two of you developed for Milbank. Unfortunately, all that technology belongs to Milbank. All their proprietary models are based on the designs you two helped develop. You might not think that is fair, but all your designs and technology are now their property."

Jeffrey did not agree. "We have plans to develop totally new products."

Noah shook his head no. "They might be totally new, but they'll still be based on the technology for which Milbank has the patents. Many of those patents are still good for many years to come."

Jeffrey did not give up easily. "We plan to develop a whole new technology!"

"That's a noble plan. But based on the present technology, it will take years and years to develop. Even then, it still has to be perfected to a degree so it is ready for production. I have great faith in both your abilities. But unless you can unleash some project like NASA, you're setting yourselves up for failure. Why go there? Why not come work for me? I can use you both. I can make good use of your talents. I would love to have guys like you on my team."

Unfortunately, Jason and Jeffrey were stubborn and hung onto their plans. Their success in the past made them overestimate their ability to develop a whole new technology. Their belief in their ability to develop a new process rubbed off on Sebastian "Sid" Caruso. Sid was head of a brand-new venture capital fund in Silicon Valley. He was looking for the golden egg that would help put his fund on the map.

The following months brought disappointment after disappointment. They were eating through cash at an alarming rate. Each sign of a breakthrough raised false hopes, only to wind up to be a dead end. Reluctantly, Sid informed them his fund would no longer pour money into the project.

Jason considered putting up more of his own money but Caroline persuaded him to face reality.

While this was going on they received the shocking news. Noah had suffered a stroke and was in critical condition in the Clinique Sainte Claire, a hospital close to Zermatt. He had been staying at his chalet when he was struck by a massive stroke.

By the next afternoon, Jason and Caroline were on a plane to Switzerland. Kitty had asked to come along to help Caroline, who was a basket case. Caroline could not accept that Noah, who had been a giant figure for all of her life, was lying in critical condition in a hospital far from home.

XLII

When the Swiss nurse ushered them into Noah's room, they were relieved to see he was still alive and conscious. All the tubes and wires attached to him worried them, but in a soft, frail voice Noah greeted them with, "Don't look so sad. Despite all these things they have running in and out of me, you'll have to suffer with me for a while longer. I'm not dead yet."

Caroline broke for the bed. She was careful not to disturb any of the tubes or wires but she had to touch Noah. "Dad, you scared us so much! The plane ride took forever. We were so worried."

Again, in a weak voice, Noah assured her he was not yet gone. He did not mention he had no feeling at all in his left side and his vision was somewhat blurry.

For three days they watched Noah's progress. Slowly his vision returned and his speech improved, but his left side did not. On the third day they were happily surprised to find him sitting up in bed. All the wires from his monitor had been removed. Noah brought up the subject of going home, and Jason carefully hinted that it would be impossible for him to return to his apartment and live by himself with only his housekeeper to take care of him.

That evening, back in their hotel, Jason, Caroline, and Kitty spent a long time discussing what to do. Jason and Caroline were all for getting Noah into a comfortable assisted living facility. The big question remained where. Caroline wanted him somewhere close to them in New York, but Jason was sure they would never get Noah to move anywhere far from his office in Chicago. Kitty disagreed with both of them. "You'll never get him to agree to move into an assisted living facility. I know him too well for that. He'll feel deprived of his freedom. To him it would be like being in prison."

Jason jumped all over his mother. "What else do you suggest? The man has had a serious stroke, and the doctors told me his entire left side will remain paralyzed. He can't take care of himself. We have no choice; he has to go to an assisted living facility. There are some really nice ones, and he can afford the best."

The next day, during their visit to the hospital, Jason explained to his father that they felt it would be best if he would go back home to a nice apartment in an assisted living facility. He wanted to know if Noah would rather be near Caroline and him in New York or return to the Chicago area. The conversation upset Noah and he was clearly agitated. His only response was, "I guess that will be up to you all. You're probably right; my active life is sort of played out."

Kitty did not like where this was going. She got up and announced she had to make a call. "While you three figure out if it's going to be the New York area or Chicago, I'll go down the hall to make a few calls."

After she left the room, she went to the nurses' station and asked if she could speak to the attending physician for the patient in Room 309. The nurse on duty spoke fluent English and was happy to escort her to Dr. Mergenthaler's office.

Kitty introduced herself as Mrs. Housten, and Dr. Mergenthaler assumed she was Noah's wife. Kitty was relieved that the doctor was also fluent in English and he was willing to go into detail about Noah's condition. "The stroke left him paralyzed on the left side. The right side has also been affected but that is not too severe and should recover in time. Actually, he is lucky; there was no other damage, and his speech, memory, hearing, and eyesight are all okay. The main trouble is his mental condition. He is very depressed. Like all men he is worried about his sexuality, and he is worried he can no longer perform. Apparently, he was told yesterday he would be placed in an assistant living facility, and he finds that difficult to accept. He realizes he is handicapped and can no longer take care of himself and that terrifies him. When you get back to the United States, I recommend you get him some counseling to help him get over this feeling of uselessness." Kitty thanked the doctor for taking the time to talk to her and returned to Noah's room.

When she returned to the room, she saw that Noah looked devastated. Gone was the enthusiasm with which he had greeted them the day before. Kitty turned to Jason and Caroline. "You two excuse yourselves and step outside for a while. I have something to discuss with your father."

When her "kids" had left the room, she turned to Noah. "Stop looking like your world has ended. Calm down, just lay back and relax." When Noah laid back and put his head on the pillows, she sat down next to the bed. To Noah's huge surprise, she slipped her hand under the sheet and down into his pajama pants.

"What the hell are you doing?" Noah was shocked; he had no idea what she was doing. Kitty's hand closed around his penis, and as Noah protested once more, she gently started rubbing her hand back and forth.

"Relax. I spoke to the doctor and he said this would be good for you. It will help get you out of the damn depressed state you're in."

"Kitty, we can't do this! Why are you touching me there?"

Kitty continued stroking his penis. "Close your eyes and lay back and enjoy!"

Noah was relieved that he could feel himself getting aroused. It was one of the things he was worried about. He had not dared ask the doctor. He was too embarrassed to discuss sex and whether it would still be possible. He no longer told Kitty to stop.

When Noah had finished, Kitty got up and went into the small attached bathroom to get a towel. When she returned, she pushed the sheet back and wiped Noah clean. She covered him back up with the sheet and said, "Well, it still works. That is one less worry for you, and for me."

Noah did not know if he should be embarrassed or what. "I guess I should say thank you. But why do that for me?"

"In case you never noticed, I still like you a lot, you old goat! And whether you like it or not, I'm taking you back home to my house. I want you back."

Noah did not believe what he heard. "You want me to go home with you?"

"Yes. If Caroline can get her man back after all those years, I want mine back too."

"But aren't you still mad that I hurt you?"

"That was long ago. We'll have plenty of time to discuss who was at fault. I've known for a long time that I was not blameless. But for now, let's concentrate on getting you comfortably settled in my house. We're lucky everything still works. We'll have a lot of fun together."

Noah was still not sure of what was happening. "Kitty, are you sure? I'm an invalid now. It is great that you're willing to take me to your house. But I don't deserve your sympathy. The kids will put me in an assisted living place, and they'll take care of me."

"Over my dead body. You will not go to any assisted living facility! I want you home with me. Stop referring to yourself as an invalid. There is nothing wrong with your mind, and that's what counts. Sure, when I fell in love with you, you had a great athletic body. But it was what's in your head that attracted me most, and that is still all there. Noah, the flame has always been smoldering. I did not have the courage to tell you, but hear this now. The flame is back."

Kitty had never seen Noah cry. He was not the type of man who showed his emotions easily. But this was too much. The fear of being locked up in an assisted living apartment was gone. Best of all, Kitty wanted him back. *Why hadn't he tried to win her back? She was always in the back of his mind. Was it true? Did she really still love him?*

"Kitty, can you come over here? I want to kiss you."

It was the response Kitty had hoped for. She leaned over the bed to kiss Noah, expertly avoiding his paralyzed left side. The doctor had told her it would be good for Noah to feel things on his right-side. She made sure he could feel as much of her body as possible as she pressed against him. As they kissed, Kitty heard the music she had longed for. "Kitty, I love you. I've never really loved anyone else."

Noah and Kitty were so involved with each other they did not hear Jason and Caroline come back into the room. They looked at each other, not knowing what to think. Jason cleared his throat loud enough for Kitty to hear. Unapologetically, she straightened up. "What's the matter? Never seen two people kiss before?"

Caroline had clapped her hand over her mouth when she first saw Kitty and Noah in an embrace. When Kitty spoke, she moved her hand down and clapped. "I think I'm seeing something great. I never dreamed I would ever witness this. This is so great!" She flew into Kitty's arms. "Does this mean what I hope it does? Are the two of you back together? Oh, Mom, say you're back with Noah, back with Dad."

"Yes. Noah is coming home with me. We'll be living together in Bayville. Jason, don't stand there gaping at us. We're your mother and father, and we're allowed to kiss."

Jason recovered quickly and he laughed. "Go right ahead. I love to see it. I can't remember ever seeing my mom and dad kissing, but this could not have come at a better time. I think both of you can use some support, and it looks to me this is a good match. I have made arrangements to get Dad out of this hospital and on a plane back home. It makes me very happy to change his destination to Chicago."

XLIII

Josephine's graduation was at the end of June, and she was worried neither her parents nor her grandparents would be able to attend. She was aware her father was having a hard time trying to keep his failing venture afloat, but she had hoped that even if he could not take the time to make the trip, her mom would come by herself. She had not been home since her grandmother and grandfather reunited. But even though she knew Noah was recovering amazingly well from his stroke, she doubted he was up to coming to California, and she thought Kitty would not leave him with a stranger.

When Caroline called to tell her all four of them would be coming, she was ecstatic. Caroline told her Noah was getting around very well in an electric wheelchair, and this would be the first time since he started therapy that he would be traveling in his plane.

Caroline told Josephine Noah said, "Even if they have to carry me on a stretcher, I will not miss my granddaughter's graduation." He insisted Jason take time off. A break would do him good, and he could not miss his only daughter's graduation. It was only May, but arrangements were already made for Noah and Kitty to fly to New York to pick up Jason and Caroline before proceeding on to San Francisco. During the call, Josephine did not tell her mother about David.

Several months earlier, she had met David. David was a classmate. They had seen each other on campus but never met. Josephine told her roommate Mandy about this handsome guy she had seen on campus. About the third time Josephine mentioned seeing this positively dreamy guy, Mandy set out to arrange a meeting. When she could not find anybody who might know him, she decided to act on her own.

Josephine had told her where she had seen this David fellow, so she went there and waited for him to appear. The first time it failed, but the second time she hit pay dirt. She couldn't miss him; he was indeed very handsome. Josephine had described him to a T. When he walked by her, Mandy stopped him. "Excuse me, can I ask you a question?"

"Sure, what would you like to know?"

"Do you have a girlfriend?"

David burst out laughing. "You're not the shyest gal on campus, are you? But you're pretty darn cute. Are you going to ask me to go with you to a party? I'm in."

"It's not for me. I'm asking for my roommate."

"Oh, sure. Where have I heard that one before? Come on, don't back out. I said I'd go out with you."

"Thanks, that would be great. But it really is for my roommate. She keeps talking about you. She says you're dreamy. You could do worse; she is a damn good-looking girl. Notice I'm not talking about her personality. That's code for 'my homely roommate.' No, this girl is terrific. She is my roommate and best friend. She's a little on the tall side, but so are you."

"Okay, I'm up for an adventure. When do I get to meet this wonderful roommate of yours?"

"You passed my personal test; I'll arrange a blind date."

"And what was that test, if I may ask?"

"You did not ask if she was African American like me before you said yes."

David had to laugh again. "Okay, fair test. But I had passed before. Don't I get credit for saying I would love to go to a party with you? By the way, I still would. Now I would like to ask you a question. Can I bring a friend along for you? Like I said, you're pretty cute, and spunky—in a good way. I would like you to meet my best friend. He's not my roommate now but we roomed together during our freshman and sophomore years."

"Yeah, that would be fun."

"Here is a test for you."

"You mean do I mind going out with a white guy? Don't worry, the answer is no."

"Nope, that was not my question. My friend's is African American like you. Well sort of. His father is an African-American doctor here in San Francisco. His Mom was from England. Unfortunately, she is no longer with us. When she passed away two years ago, Keith moved back home to live with his father."

"That is great! My folks are both doctors. We'll have bushels of things to talk about. You think this coming Saturday night will be okay?"

"Perfect. I'm sure Keith hasn't made other plans."

"Shall we plan on a movie?"

"Come on, not that! What's wrong with some conversation? It will be much more fun if Keith and I pick you gals up for dinner and we go someplace where the four of us can talk. How else will we get to know each other?"

"You said you had a question for me."

"Yeah, I was going to ask if it would be okay for the four of us to go out for dinner, but that has already been settled. We'll pick you up this Saturday evening."

Her little adventure had turned out much better than she expected, and Mandy raced back to their apartment to tell Josephine. Josephine responded with, "You what?"

"I fixed you up with dreamy. You should be happy."

"Wow, you've got some nerve. You walked right up to him and asked?"

"Yes, he's a great sport. Right away he said yes. He didn't say anything like, 'I have to see her first,' or, 'I don't even know you.' He just said yes. He was okay with it. By the way, you weren't lying; the guy is drop-dead gorgeous."

"Mandy, you're amazing! I wish I had your courage. I would never dare do such a thing!"

"I never thought it would turn out so well. It was worth a try; but to get an immediate yes and to get a date for myself at the same time? That's like hitting the jackpot. I'm amazed a good-looking guy like that isn't already spoken for. And how about him fixing me up with this Keith, the doctor's son? I hope he's halfway decent."

Josephine, ever the cautious one, said, "I hope money doesn't get in the way."

"It won't if you shut up about it. They'll assume something when they see this apartment, but they are picking us up, so they won't see either of our cars. Our cars are the main turnoff for all guys except the gold diggers. We'll just be careful to keep them out of the conversation."

On Saturday night, David and Keith came to get the girls at their Gateway apartment in San Mateo. Josephine and Mandy were relieved the men did not seem the least bit impressed by the luxurious apartment building in which the girls lived. Their only comment when they entered the apartment was, "Nice place. You lived here long?" Mandy told them they had moved here after their sophomore year.

David said that he and Keith had shared a cute little place in Nob Hill until Keith moved back in with his dad. Nonchalantly, David mentioned that a year ago he moved into an apartment in Lands End. The girls glanced at each other, thinking it was a poor joke. Lands End was one of the most expensive places in Pacifica.

When they got to David's car, they realized he must not have been kidding about his apartment. David's car was a Porsche Panamera Turbo S. They felt a little silly having worried what the guys would think if they heard that both of them drove Ford Mustangs.

Keith had booked a table at Casa Flores in Nob Hill. When they were shown to their table, it was obvious the men were no strangers to the place. Vanessa and Julian, their hosts, welcomed them back and called them both by their first names.

The dinner was superb. By far the best either of the girls had had in San Francisco. But what made the evening for all four of them was the conversation. They seemed very comfortable with each other right off the bat.

David finally explained why. "When Mandy accosted me on campus," everybody laughed, knowing he used that word to tease her, "I was totally up for an adventure. I told her truthfully that I do not have a serious girlfriend. I do date a lot, but I always have this uncomfortable feeling that girls like my father's money more than they like me. You might as well know, my dad is Gilford Schroeder. He is head of a big hedge fund down in the valley. A lot of people are jealous of him and try to belittle him by referring to him as nouveau riche. Well, maybe he shows off his success by throwing money around. But that does not take away from the fact that he came up from nothing to be one of the richest men in this state. As you can tell by the car I drive, I'm one of the main beneficiaries of his desire to show off his wealth.

"Keith's dad has not done too badly either. He lives around the corner in one of the nicest houses here in Pacific Heights. That's probably why Keith and I became such good friends. Between us, we make no excuses that our dads are rich and spoil us rotten."

Mandy was about to interrupt him but David held up his hand. "Let me finish and tell you both what I know about you. When your father runs a large hedge fund, you have access to a research department filled with very clever people. I asked them for some help and had little trouble finding out all about you two. So Keith and I know you're not here because of money."

Mandy wanted to know some more about Keith's family. "David told me your mother was English. Tell us how she met your dad here in the United States."

"Okay, but first let me brag a little about my dad. Dad was a big football star here at Stanford. He was an All American top draft pick and got a huge bonus for signing a professional contract. Unfortunately, or fortunately, as it turned out, Dad got badly injured during his third year as a professional. Rather than feel sorry for himself, he went back to school. He had enough money to finance his way all through medical school and beyond. Now he is a prominent cardiologist here in San Francisco. His is quite a success story for a man of color."

"Sounds like my parents," Mandy said. "Despite everything, both of them fought their way to the top. But what about your mom?"

"Mom came to America on her own when she was barely twenty years old. She got a job in a hospital in San Antonio, Texas. She met my dad there. He was an intern at the time. She told me it was love at first sight. After a whirlwind courtship they were married less than six months after they met. Unfortunately, she died too young. Dad has never really recovered, so I moved back home to be with him."

When the girls got back to their apartment, Josephine could not stop talking about David. "Isn't he the greatest? Mandy, I'm so happy you fixed me up with him. He asked me to meet him Tuesday evening at The Axe & Palm on campus. We'll have dinner together. What about Keith? Do you like him? You two have a lot in common, your parents being doctors and such."

"Josephine, I know you well enough that 'and such' does not mean that we're both black."

"Oops, that was stupid of me. Of course not! I mean your parents and his dad working their way up from an unlikely background to become doctors."

"Yeah, I like him. He's okay. But as you know, there is this guy back home I have a serious crush on. After we graduate, I'll go back home and see what develops."

XLIV

The Axe & Palm stays open late, and David and Josephine were among the last to leave. Josephine was head over heels in love with David, and she jumped at his invitation to come see his Land's End apartment. Mandy was skeptical. She did not think it was a good idea. "You hardly know the fellow."

"We accepted their invitation to go out to dinner. We knew even less about them at the time."

"That was different. The two of us were together and we went to a public place. If they had asked us to meet them at his apartment, I would have refused."

Starry-eyed, Josephine waved off Mandy's warning, and the following Saturday evening she drove out to Pacifica to meet David in his Lands End apartment.

The interior of the apartment was much less fancy than it had been described to her but the view of the ocean more than made up for that, particularly the sunset. That was spectacular. David had soft music on and had drinks and little snacks ready when she arrived.

David showed her the pool area and the well-equipped gym. After that, he suggested they take his car and drive down to the beach. They took a long walk along the water and David held her tightly, his hand occasionally rubbing along her lower back.

Back in the apartment, they fell into a slow dance on his balcony. David kissed her and suggested they go back in. He led her to the big circular couch and they started making out. Josephine enjoyed David touching her and she passionately kissed him. She did not object when David unbuttoned her blouse and put his hand inside her bra. David pushed her back on the couch and laid on top of her. Josephine continued kissing him. Her nipples became very firm and he could feel her responding to his touch. When his hand slid down and he started pulling her skirt up, Josephine resisted. "David, let's not. I like it when you stroke my breasts but please don't go there." David ignored her and pulled her skirt up. "David, don't! I asked you to stop; I don't like you to touch me there."

With his left hand, David tightened his grip around her and with his right hand, he forcefully pulled her skirt up to her midriff. Josephine panicked. "No, David, no! Get off me." David did not stop. He tore her panties off and crabbed her crotch. She could feel his fingers exploring her vagina. Josephine's legs were kicking wildly; she pushed against his chest, screaming, "Get off me! David, don't! Please don't!"

David's body was too heavy for Josephine to push him away. His left hand remained like a vise around her shoulders while he tried to get his pants open. Josephine thought she was going to faint she was so scared. Then she saw a vision of Kristy in front of her eyes and clearly heard: "Fight, damn it, fight! He is evil!" Her strong, athletic body sprang into action. One hand broke free; she clawed at his cheek and drew blood. David's hand went up to his bleeding cheek and that released his grip on her. Josephine pushed one foot into the couch and pushed hard. With David still on top of her, she rolled off the couch. When they hit the floor she kept on rolling. David fell off her and Josephine got up and raced for the door. On the way she grabbed her pocketbook off the table and flew out the door. Half-dressed, she raced for her car and sped off before David appeared outside the building.

In a completely disheveled state, Josephine fell into Mandy's arms. "Josephine, what happened? Did you crash your car?"

"No . . . David tried to rape me!"

Mandy held Josephine a little longer in her arms, then asked, "Tried, or did?"

"I fought him off. No, he only tried. Mandy . . . he got his hand on my vagina. He tried to rape me!"

"I'll call the police."

"Don't!"

"We have to. You can't let him get away with it. We must report it. It's criminal."

"I know that, but how can I prove it? He'll deny it."

"Let him try. Look at you! I'll testify."

"It won't work. Let me just talk to the university officials. They'll tell me what to do."

Talking to the university officials turned out to be a dead end. The lady whom Josephine spoke to was very sympathetic, but of little help. She told Josephine, "You have no injuries to show what happened. From what you tell me, the only one injured was David. That does not help your case; it might even hurt it. I believe you, but my hands are tied."

Mandy was not about to let it go. She asked Morgan and Barbara to come to their apartment to discuss the matter. Barbara was sure there were other girls who had been attacked by David. "I'm sure there must be dozens of girls who fell into that bastard's trap. Give me some time and I'll round them up." Morgan had an idea. "When you get a few girls who have been attacked by David to help us, I have a plan to get him."

Barbara turned out to be a great detective, and a persuasive one at that. In a few weeks she found nine girls who admitted that David had raped them. Best of all, they were willing to help punish him.

Morgan staked out The Axe & Palm for several days. When David entered at lunchtime, she called the twelve others and they arrived carrying the signs they had prepared. All twelve of them carried big signs with red letters spelling out "I am a rapist". They marched around the table David was sitting at. While holding the sign in one hand they beat with a wooden spoon on a metal cup hung round their waist. It did not take long before many in the room, filled with the lunch crowd, started clapping in rhythm with them. David dropped the hamburger he was eating and fled out the door. The twelve girls ran behind him. Things went better than they had hoped. At least fifty students followed them; half were boys. The crowd surrounded David's car and started banging on it with anything they could find. David took off, nearly hitting a girl as he tore out of the parking lot.

A week later, Josephine was served with a subpoena. David was suing her for slander. Keith was called to testify on behalf of David. David's lawyer had not expected all the girls who had participated in the scene at The Axe & Palm to drop their anonymity and agree to testify on behalf of Josephine.

Keith told the court David always had plenty of dates. Many of them would gladly stay the night. He knew because when they still lived together he would go home to give David some privacy. He said there was absolutely no reason David would have to resort to rape. Girls, very pretty girls, would always be happy to have sex with him.

Each one of the girls was challenged by David's lawyer. If David had raped them, why did they not report it? Each time the story was the same. They were ashamed, and anyway, no one would believe them. You could not win against a rich, popular guy like David.

This changed when Ellie Abrams testified. Ellie told the court she was only seventeen when David got her drunk and raped her. She had just arrived at school. And, as a freshman, she was delighted to be asked out by an upperclassman. After it happened, she was scared stiff. When she confided in her roommate, her roommate told her that because she had gotten drunk, the university would most likely expel her. So she kept quiet and never reported she had been raped by David. She was a sophomore now and had the same roommate. They had since learned that getting drunk was not a violation for which you got expelled. It was her roommate who spoke to Barbara and after that, persuaded Ellie to speak up. During her testimony, Ellie pointed at a girl sitting in back of the court. "That's Peggy, my roommate."

David's lawyer leaned over to speak to David's father, who had accompanied his son. After a brief discussion, the lawyer addressed the court. "Your Honor, my client has decided to agree to drop the charges."

Josephine's lawyer rose. "Your Honor, this case should be referred to the District Attorney. That young man should be charged with statutory rape. Ellie Abrams was only seventeen last year when she was raped by David Schroeder."

The judge was annoyed. "Counselor, I do not need you to advise me on the law. We are capable of handling this without your help."

When Josephine, Mandy, and the rest of the girls were leaving the courthouse, Keith and his father approached them. He had not played football for many years but Keith's father, Dr. Newton, was still an imposing figure. He towered over Keith by at least half a foot. He singled Josephine out and spoke directly to her. "I'm sorry I failed you and the other ladies also. As a doctor, I should have recognized that bad streak in David's personality. Of course I was aware that David took advantage of women. But it seemed to me they were always willing partners infatuated by his wealth. Expensive cars, beautiful apartment, the works. He spent freely on his dates, and I thought the ladies loved it. I failed to see that sex was not enough for him. He had to dominate. He got his sexual satisfaction by complete domination over a woman. If she resisted him, so much the better. He is one sick puppy. If I had recognized this at an earlier stage I could have saved you from the nightmare you had to endure. I'm truly sorry."

None of the girls knew how to respond. Spontaneously, young Ellie Abrams stepped forward. She went up to Dr. Newton and pulled his head down and kissed him on the cheek. "Thank you for saying that, Doctor. Calling him a sick person makes me feel less cheap about what happened. Now I know I was attacked by a sicko. And as drunk as I was, I wasn't just leading a man on and getting what I deserved."

The university conducted its own investigation, and David was expelled two weeks before graduation. Not much longer after that, the DA charged him with statutory rape and multiple charges of sexual assault.

XLV

Graduation was both exciting and sad. Josephine and Mandy had met each other's parents several times during parents' weekend, but Morgan and Barbara's parents had never visited Stanford. This would be the first time all four of them would have their parents on campus together so they could finally meet. That was exciting, but it was also the time when the Four Musketeers would have to part. Saying good-bye after sharing every new experience together for the last four years would be very hard.

Mandy arranged a lunch for all four of them with their parents at Joya. Joya is right in the middle of Palo Alto. She chose Joya because of the great food and because it was near the university, easy to get to for everyone. She also took into consideration that Noah would be in a wheelchair. The restaurant assured her that would not be a problem. Joya was wheelchair accessible, and Noah could be dropped off right in front. They would make sure no cars were parked at the curb in front of their restaurant.

Josephine was happy to see how proud both Morgan and Barbara were of their parents and how easily they carried on a conversation with her parents and grandparents. More important than that was how Barbara's, and of course, Morgan's parents would interact with Mandy's folks. The Four Musketeers were delighted that everyone got along just fine.

Mandy had been watching very carefully how Barbara's parents and hers would get along. She said nothing, but watched as Barbara's father selected a seat next to her father's. The two of them got into a conversation and talked for most of the meal.

Towards the end of the lunch, Morgan's father got up and said he wanted to make a toast. "It's no secret that my wife and I did not particularly like rich folks before our daughter came to Stanford. In the four years our Morgan has been here, we learned that we had a problem. We had only met the wrong rich people. They are not the norm. They are the exception. And then there are also the exceptions that go the other way. The folks who are truly good people. My daughter was blessed. She roomed with two girls whose families represent the good exceptions.

"My wife and I never imagined there were people who had money and remained such good people, such exceptional people. Morgan and Josephine's families have brought this sense of decency over into the next generation. Because they did, our daughters became close friends. They did not care who had money or what color their skin was. They loved each other. Seeing this happen was a gift to my wife and me. We were not born with much; we had to work hard. But we have been blessed that our daughter became part of this amazing foursome. I want to thank God for this blessing.

"I love all of you but I have to single out one person. He represents the very best. I don't want to embarrass you, Mr. Housten Sr. You might be in a wheelchair, but to me you are still my hero. You are a great man, and I look up to you. You are my hero, a giant among men. You changed me from a bitter man into a grateful man. We all know what you did for our daughter. But you did much more than that. You treat your employees like human beings. You pay them a good wage so they can live a decent life. Coming here to see our daughter graduate is a humbling experience for my wife and me. I've looked forward to it, but I have just as much looked forward to meeting you and your great family. I just want to give you a hug. Is that okay?"

Barbara's father was the first up on his feet. Clapping loudly, he kept repeating, "Amen to that."

When the clapping finally stopped, Mandy's father rose to speak. Dr. Jackson was a handsome man and from having addressed many medical conferences, he was comfortable speaking on his feet. "Mandy grew up in a mostly white suburb of Detroit. Because both my wife and I are doctors, it was not too difficult for her to be the only black girl in class. That would not have been the case in many other places. I know some of you come from areas where black folks are not accepted as equal. Black and white don't mix well in many places of our great country.

"I hasten to say that this is not always due to feelings on the white side. Both races have a lot to learn. That's why I want to add to what Barbara's father so eloquently expressed. It has truly been a joy for my wife and me to see our daughters develop a deep friendship. I have heard them called the Four Musketeers. These four young women have cut through the barriers of race and social position and they accept each other for who they are as a person and nothing else. That is inspiring. It gives me hope that someday that will be the norm in this country. Let's raise our glasses in a toast to our daughters and express the hope that they are the vanguard. That we may learn from them."

XLVI

After she packed up and was ready to fly home with her parents and grandparents, Josephine had one more problem. What to do with her car. Jason had been adamant. He would not let her drive the car home by herself. She asked her mom if she would drive with her but Noah had a much better idea. "Sell the damn thing. I have been wondering what to give you for your graduation. That solves it. I'll buy you a new one when we get home."

"This car is barely three years old! If you buy me a new one, I'll really be known as a spoiled brat."

"Fine, live with it. There are worse things than being a spoiled brat. If you move in with your parents in New York City, you might not even need a car. We'll talk about it. But for now, just sell the thing."

The evening before they were scheduled to fly back to New York, Josephine mentioned to her grandfather, "It's funny, my father and mother are my biological parents, and you and Granma are my real grandparents, yet none of you are married."

That gave Noah an idea. At dinner he proposed. "What if we make a stop in Las Vegas and have a double wedding?"

Caroline and Kitty agreed immediately. They thought it was a great idea. Jason laughed at his father. "What made you think of that? Tired of living in sin?"

"Actually, Jo Jo brought it up. She thought it was strange her parents and grandparents were not married. I agreed with her. I can call the pilots right now and ask them to file a flight plan to Vegas in the morning. Those two will love it. I'll tell them we'll stay the night. Caroline, do you mind booking some rooms for us? Once we're married, you and Jason and Kitty and I can sleep in double rooms without embarrassing Jo Jo. Don't forget the pilots and the flight attendant. We'll need four singles; three for them and one for Jo Jo."

Jo Jo did not think the crack about double rooms was funny. "You might not realize it, but the four of you getting married is a very meaningful graduation present. I'm almost twenty-four, and my family is finally getting together. I don't think I've ever seen Mom happier, and that smile on Granma's face is not just because I just graduated. Call me sentimental, that's okay, but I feel more comfortable having a normal family. It gives me the stability I never felt as a child."

Vegas was a ball. It started in a fun way when Jason arranged for an Elvis wedding package for the double wedding. The pink Cadillac that came with the package was only used by Caroline and Jason. It was too cumbersome for Noah. He and Kitty followed the Cadillac in a SUV. After the wedding, Caroline, Jason, and their parents retreated to the hotel to relax around the pool. Roger, the flight attendant, and the two pilots took Josephine along to go hotel hopping. Roger turned out to be an excellent guide. He had been to Vegas numerous times and this was Josephine's first time. Roger told them it was well worthwhile to go out to the Grand Canyon and the Hoover Dam. Nobody minded that they would have to extend their stay in Las Vegas by a full day to take in those sights. The next day, they rented a helicopter big enough to take all eight of them on the excursion.

Josephine would have loved to stay another day, but it was time to go home. The plane first flew to New York to drop off Jason, Caroline, and Josephine. After that they flew to Chicago. From there, Kitty and Noah would go home to Bayville by car.

XLVII

There was a letter waiting for them when Kitty and Noah arrived home. The envelope did not have a return address, and the stamp revealed the letter was posted in Australia. It was addressed to Mrs. Kitty Housten. The address was handwritten in a childish scrawl.

Kitty could hardly wait to find out what it was all about. She knew no one in Australia, and could not think of any of her friends who might have recently moved there.

The envelope contained three handwritten pages. Kitty started reading.

Dear Mrs. Housten,

My name is Jennifer Douglas, and I owe you an apology. I'm the woman who broke up your marriage, and I am terribly ashamed of what I did.

I had just broken off an abusive relationship when I was hired by your husband's company to be his personal assistant. I was aware that he was in a very vulnerable state of mind due to the things that had happened to a storage depot of the company in Rotterdam. He took everything that happened there personally, and I was hired in part to help cheer him up. Mrs. Housten, I did not mean to let it happen, but our relationship became more and more intimate as time went on. I tried to stop myself, but I could not help it. I never intended to let our relationship get out of hand, but I fell in love with your husband. I must assure you. Please believe me, it was never him. It was all my doing, I led him on. I had to literally seduce him on that first night he slept with me.

After we were married, I betrayed him. I loved him dearly, and if it had not been for my weakness with drugs, I would never have betrayed him. But I did. It all started when we became friends with Arnold Thomson, the star outfielder of the New York Yankees. He became part of our circle of friends, many of whom would spend the weekend at our house. While your husband was traveling, Arnold introduced a group of us to cocaine. Unlike the others, I became addicted to the stuff after the second or third time he brought it to our house. Noah was completely oblivious as to what was going on, even though I was heavily into the stuff. One time while Noah was once again traveling, Arnold was staying at the house for the weekend.

This time he refused to give me any of his cocaine. I badly needed a fix, and I begged him to give me some. He refused, and I was desperate. He was the only one I could get cocaine from. I had no contact with his dealers, and no idea where else to get it. Finally he consented, but only on the condition that I sleep with him. This went on for two consecutive nights. When Noah returned home, he somehow found out what happened.

He kicked us both out of the house. I was unaware Arnold had been dropped from the Yankees for his excessive drug use. We floated around a while from city to city until Arnold got arrested for dealing. He still had his contacts in New York and had been acting as sort of their agent. I drifted on. By now I knew how to get cocaine. It's relatively easy to find a source in any city, big or small. To support my habit, I went back to work. I'm quite qualified, and I got a job as secretary in a small company. I had become rather reckless in buying the stuff and I got caught in a sting operation. I was lucky. As a first-time offender, I only got probation.

After that, no one would hire me and I took up prostitution. At first that paid well, but again I became reckless. This time they threw the book at me, and I went to jail for a year. In jail they cleaned me up, but when I got out, I went right back to using drugs. My looks had gone down the drain and I could do no better than becoming a common whore doing cheap tricks. I picked up men in dingy bars and standing on street corners.

It did not take long before I was arrested again. I was a real mess. They told me I had the right to make one call before they dragged me off to jail. I had only one number in my clouded drug head. It was Noah's cell. I was lucky he answered. I told him I would kill myself if they locked me up again; could he send someone to help? I never expected that he would come immediately.

He arrived with his lawyers in tow and with the help of some high-priced local attorneys, they got me out. No jail time. No nothing. The police released me into his care. He had me brought to a rehab center. One of those fancy ones that advertise on TV. When I was discharged from there I received the following message from him.

"The next step is up to you. You can regress and die on the street or you can rebuild your life. Enclosed is a thousand bucks. Check into a hotel and contact me. Tell me what you want to do. If you choose to get back your life, I'll help you. You will receive a plane ticket to Australia. There will be a job waiting there for you in my branch office. No one there will know about your past. You'll come highly recommended by me. They'll have no choice but to hire you. I'll make sure you have enough cash to tide you over for the first couple of months. If you choose to go back to using that filth, don't ever contact me again. If you do go to Australia, we should avoid all future contact. If you're wondering why I'm doing this, it's because I owe you one. You rescued me out of a deep depression. I was at a low point of my life and without your support I could never have rebuilt my company."

Dear Mrs. Housten, I did a very bad thing, but how could I not fall in love with that wonderful man? Please forgive me. I swear I'll avoid all contact with Noah. I love him enough to do what is best for him; I'll stay out of his life. I will be forever grateful that he gave me back mine.

Respectfully yours,

Jennifer Douglas

Kitty sat for a long time staring at the three pages lying on her lap. She could not decide if she should show the letter to Noah. Finally she decided he deserved to read it. He deserved to know Jennifer had told her she was the one who instigated their affair and that she actually had to seduce him to get him to sleep with her. It would not hurt to let him know she now knew what he had done for that woman. She planned to tell him she was impressed with how gracefully he handled the situation. She went into the bedroom where Noah was resting after the long trip. "Here, read this," was all she said when she handed him the three pages. She sat down and patiently waited for Noah to finish reading.

When Noah put down the letter he said, "The fact remains I cheated on you, and that is still troubling me. I know we've made up. You've been absolutely wonderful about it, and I know I now love you more than ever. But the fact remains, I cheated."

"Before you put on your sack cloth and ashes, let's discuss this. After our divorce, I realized I was partly responsible for the breakup of our marriage. In the first place I, and not Jennifer, should have been there for you during that horrible time when everyone, and even you yourself, tried to blame you for what happened in Rotterdam."

Noah tried to interrupt her but she hushed him up. "Let me explain some more. I was not a very good wife. I loved you dearly, but there was no passion in our marriage. The occasional time I let you touch me I held back. I did not enjoy it. You deserved better than that. You were young and had normal sexual desires, but I did not respond in a normal way. After our divorce, I saw a psychiatrist who helped me work through my problem. What I'm about to tell you must stay between us. Promise?"

"Of course. I never knew you went to a psychiatrist."

"No one knows accept me and the psychiatrist. But let me tell you the full story. When I was sixteen, my nineteen-year-old cousin raped me."

"He what?"

"Raped me! Yes, he raped me. But let me tell you how it happened. I was staying at my aunt's house, and my cousin was home for the summer. Everyone in the family knew I had a crush on him. As a kid I followed him around like a puppy. When he was younger he considered me a real pest.

"By the time I was sixteen, my skinny frame had filled out very nicely, and I was proud of my body. Lately, at sweet sixteen parties, boys had been paying a lot of attention to me. When they danced with me some of them tried to touch my breasts. I liked over-hearing them when they discussed what they called my great set of boobs. I was not promiscuous, but I did not mind making out with a date.

"It bothered me that my cousin, the big shot home from college, still considered me a child. I was out to show him I was all grown up. Everybody was out one afternoon except my cousin Eric and me. I suggested we go for a swim; my aunt's house had a nice fenced-in pool in the back of the house. I put on my brand-new bikini, hoping he would notice my sexy curves. He noticed, and I pranced around like a cheap little flirt. My breasts just about burst out of my skimpy bikini top.

"When we went back inside I was still dripping wet and Eric offered to dry me off. I handed him my towel and he did my back. He turned me around and started on my chest. All of a sudden, something changed. He became a wild man. He ripped off my bikini top and before I could pull away he also tore off my bikini bottom. He grabbed hold of me and pushed me to the floor. I screamed. Hollered for him to stop. But he held me down tightly and raped me.

"He was rough and hurt me terribly. When he finished, I remained crumpled up on the floor. A look of horror came across Eric's face. 'Oh my God, what did I do?' he cried. He reached down to help me up. He was in a complete state of panic. 'I'm sorry . . . I did not want to do that.' He was crying even harder than I was. He grabbed hold of me. 'You could get pregnant. Quick, I have to get you into the bath!'

We raced up the stairs and filled the bathtub. I got in and he attempted to push water into my vagina. With the water still running, we did not hear my aunt arrive home. She saw my ripped bikini lying on the floor and raced up the stairs to see what was going on.

She found us in the bathroom. Me naked in the tub and Eric bent over me. The next scene was far from pretty. My aunt was furious with us but mostly with me. She never tried to find out what really happened. If she had bothered to look closely, she would have seen the bruises on my breasts. She called me a little slut. A Lolita. Much later, I went to the library to find out what that meant.

The next morning, she put me on a plane back home. She told my mom I was no longer welcome at her house because I did not know how to behave like a decent girl. I was ashamed. I blamed myself for what happened and never told anyone Eric raped me. About a week after I got back home I had my period. I knew I was not pregnant, and relished the thought that Eric would have to worry for a long time before realizing I was not expecting a child."

Noah cringed when Kitty reached the part where Eric ripped her bikini off and forced himself on her. He did not interrupt her right away, but finally said, "Why didn't you share this with me? I would have understood why it was difficult for you to accept me touching you."

"I couldn't. I could not talk about it. I tried to blot the whole thing out of my mind. Not until I went to the psychiatrist did all the details come back. She explained that I was blaming myself for something that was done to me totally against my will; blaming myself was wrong. She said I was raped. Cruelly raped by someone I trusted. Even if I was prancing around showing off my body, I did not deserve to be assaulted. According to her, every young girl has a little naughty streak in her, especially if she has just gone through puberty and is not used to having a body that attracts men. She told me I was punishing myself by refusing to enjoy being touched by a man. She sympathized with me; told me she understood it was difficult for me to have intercourse with you during our marriage. She advised me to get a boyfriend and slowly work through my problem. I couldn't do that. I wanted you back. I wanted our years of marriage back so I could make things up to you. When we were together at Caroline's wedding I wanted to ask you to stay at my house for the night. We could have slept together and made up. I didn't have the courage to do that. I did not dare ask for fear of being rebuffed. Now I can confess that during the times you came to visit Josephine I was dying to tell you how much I still loved you. This letter from Jennifer makes me hope that through all the years, the feeling was mutual."

Using his good right hand, Noah tried to push himself up into a sitting position. Kitty rushed over to help him. He said, "I might have been yearning to have you back more than you wanted me back. Give me a big kiss. I'll try to hold onto you the best I can."

They kissed for a long time until Noah said, "We've tried our best since we got back from Switzerland and making love has been wonderful. But me being a cripple doesn't help."

"Stop calling yourself a cripple! Yes, you have a handicap, but that does not have to stop us from enjoying each other to the fullest. I have attended a clinic at the hospital and learned about special positions to use if one partner is partly paralyzed. If you're not too tired from the trip, I'll show you. We can practice."

"Too tired to make love to you? Never! Show me your new magic."

Kitty quickly helped Noah out of his clothes. Next she slowly, as if doing a striptease show, removed her clothes. Noah enjoyed the show and whistled. "Man, you still have a great body."

Kitty laughed and gently lowered her naked body on top of him. She made sure most of her weight rested on his right side. She whispered, "Beauty is in the eye of the beholder."

XLVIII

Kitty and Noah slept-in pretty late the next morning. When they finally got around to having breakfast, they sat around the table giggling like two newlyweds reminiscing about their first date. Kitty speculated, "I wonder if I had been willing, whether we would have had more kids."

"You can say the same for Jason and Caroline. I doubt she will have another child at her age. I know women in their forties do become pregnant, but I don't see that as a realistic possibility."

Kitty was looking further ahead. "We'll just have to wait for Josephine to make us great-granpa and great-granma. The way you spoil your Jo Jo, that should be quite a spectacle."

Kitty raised a question that was bothering her. "I've heard rumors of what happened to Josephine a few months before graduation. Apparently a classmate attacked her while she was out on a date. I hope it doesn't affect her like it did me."

"Sweetheart, if it does, I know someone who is eminently qualified to help her. Kitty, the next time she comes to visit us, have a heart-to-heart talk with her. Break your silence on the subject. Be totally honest and explain what happened to you and how we feel about each other now. She is old enough to understand."

Noah abruptly changed the subject. "Speaking of children, I have to call Jason. He sounds so depressed whenever I have him on the phone. This will be his first full day back and I want to find out what is going on with that new venture of his. No matter what anyone says, he won't give up on that venture. From the start I told him it was much too ambitious."

When Noah called, Jason was busy on the phone trying to raise more money to keep his operation going. In half an hour he called back. He told Noah he had struck out once again and hinted he really could use Noah's help. Noah turned that around.

"Jason, I need you. Traveling back and forth to my office in Chicago is becoming too much for me. And I have also seen enough of the inside of that plane. It's more than that; I no longer want to travel and be away from your mother for any length of time. It's time for me to step down as CEO."

Not realizing where Noah was going, Jason asked, "You want me to help you find a suitable successor?"

"Not exactly. I don't need a search committee to help me find my successor. I know who I want. I will inform the board of directors I'm stepping down and the search has been completed. There always was only one candidate. That is you, son."

Jason tried his best to protest. "Come on, there are plenty of men with more experience, and they are certainly better qualified to run a huge outfit like yours."

"I have to make that judgment, and I disagree. You have the experience running an international company. Even the bad experience you suffered can be valuable in running a company. Jason, in the end, it all comes down to trust. There is nobody I trust better to take over than my own son. Please, Jason, don't turn me down!"

Noah's last sentence hit Jason hard. His dad had never pleaded with him. "You're not just saying all that because you're still depressed after your stroke?"

"In case you haven't noticed, I'm not a spring chicken anymore. All my life I pushed myself very hard. Maybe too hard; that's probably why I had a stroke. No, Jason, it is time for me to step down. And who better than my son to continue my life's work? Jason, when you left college I asked you to join me in the company. That was too soon. You have proven yourself since that time, and now the time has come to help me."

Jason couldn't get himself to tell his father how he felt. A moment ago he had felt like a complete failure, but now there was someone who still believed in him. Not just anybody. His father, an icon in his industry, trusted him to succeed him. All he could say was, "Dad, you know I talk everything over with Caroline. Let me discuss this with her."

"That's the way it should be. Take your time; I'll wait for your decision. There are no other candidates."

XLIX

It did not take Caroline long to say yes. She jumped at the opportunity. "Jason, that is terrific! It's a win-win situation. Your dad needs you, and this project of ours is dragging you down without any prospects in sight. Yes, we'll do it!"

"What about Jeffrey Milkowsky and our employees?"

"We'll take Jeffrey along with us. I'm sure there is a place for him in your father's company. As for the rest of the people, don't worry. Most of them have already left. They saw the end coming. The few loyal souls who are still with us will have no trouble finding new work. You have a lot of connections in the electronics industry. If they have trouble finding something stable, I'm sure you can help."

"What about this apartment? We have a heavy mortgage."

"Don't look for problems where there are none. Things will take care of themselves. Just tell your dad yes, and we'll see what follows next. Jason, be happy!

This is the best thing that could have happened to us. Your father is a gem. If things are difficult in the beginning, he'll be by your side. But you won't need it. Gosh, you were valedictorian of our class; two of the best colleges in America accepted you. You built a fantastic company. There is no doubt in my mind that you can handle this. Call Dad now. Say yes!"

When Jason called to say yes, Kitty grabbed the phone. "My kids are coming home! You'll have to move to Chicago. Watch out, I'll be within driving distance!"

When Noah got the phone back, Jason mentioned his concern about leaving Jeffrey behind. Noah put his mind at ease. "That is not a problem. It will be an advantage if you bring along your own chief information officer. With someone like Jeffrey at your side, you'll always be one step ahead of the competition. And you mention moving to Chicago. Of course you have to live close to our head office. I still maintain my apartment in The Streeter. That's a great location, and it's ready for you and Caroline to move in. You'll have your home office all set up and, if she wants it, there is a lovely spare room for Jo Jo. I know you'll hate selling your place on the park but The Streeter is nothing to sneeze at."

The transition at the company went smoothly. Top management was surprised at how Noah, in his position of chairman, deferred all decisions to the new CEO. On the personal side, things turned out amazingly well also. The apartment in Manhattan sold for much more than Jason had expected. After paying off the mortgage, there was enough leftover to pay off his remaining debts and give Caroline a nice budget to furnish their new home in The Streeter.

Noah's furnishings in the apartment were a little too austere for Caroline. As she told Jason, "Looks like he hardly ever entertained in here. I doubt that, except for his housekeeper, any woman ever saw the inside of the place."

By far the worst was the so-called guest room. It contained a huge king-size bed and a dresser. For the rest it was completely bare. Noah hadn't even bothered to get sheets for the bed or any kind of window dressing. Josephine was delighted; Caroline let her furnish the room completely according to her own tastes.

The bronze figurine of the DO NO EVIL monkey got a place of honor in their new living room. When Caroline saw the figurine on Jason's desk she had asked where he got it. "It's adorable. I love it; do you mind if we move it out of your office and place it on the mantel in the living room?" Jason was not sure if he should tell Caroline that Kristy had the little bronze specially made for him. He started by only telling her someone had it made for him to remind him of the horrible consequences evil deeds can have. When Caroline wanted to know who gave it to him, Jason had to tell her it was Kristy.

"Then it certainly has to come out of your office and be put in a place where people will see it." Caroline picked up the little monkey and carried it into the living room. She placed it on the mantel and said, "It's so Kristy. We have to remember her as the good person she was. She really hated evil; I'm glad she never knew what Jerry did to you."

There was a marked change in Noah's character. He was no longer the dominant, overbearing person Jason knew. Now he was happy to let Kitty take the lead. It was obvious he adored her, and everything she did was okay with him. According to Caroline, he had never been happier in his life. When she mentioned it to Jason she added, "And neither has Kitty."

To celebrate having her family together for the first time at Christmas, Kitty prepared a bountiful Christmas dinner, which she insisted on serving in her formal dining room. She had decorated the entire house and Jason, even when he was growing up, had never seen the house so festive.

After the meal, Caroline suggested they take a sentimental journey through Bayville to see the decorations on Main Street.

Main Street was deserted, and they had no problem finding a parking spot. It was bitterly cold but they did not care; they were in a great mood. Noah had no trouble keeping up. The sidewalks had been cleared and he had become an expert at steering his electric chair with his good right hand. Halfway down the street, Caroline noticed the "Going out of Business" sign on the Samson's Hardware building. Like all the other shops on Main Street the hardware store was closed for Christmas, but the lights in the store were on.

Caroline was curious and said, "I wonder if Reggie McLaughlin still works there." She wanted to go inside and inquire what had happened to her old friend.

When they went inside, she saw Reggie in the back of the store. She called out, "Hey, Reggie, remember me?"

Reggie looked up. "Caroline! Haven't seen you since that huge wedding party at your and Mrs. Housten's house. How are you?"

"Great. Couldn't be better. Do you remember Jason?"

"Well, I'll be damned, Caroline and Jason together here in Bayville. Who would have thunk it!"

Jason stepped forward with a big smile. "Shocking news, Reggie; Caroline and I are married, and we are visiting my mom and dad with our daughter, Josephine."

If Reggie had just met ET from outer space, he could not have been more surprised. "Well, I'll be damned! My two best buddies from high school, married! Come here, you two, that calls for a big hug!"

Reggie put his arms around Jason and Caroline; he just could not believe it. "Jason, I take back everything I said about you. You're not an SOB after all. All these years I have been pissed at you for not marrying Caroline, and now you did. Christ, buddy, you have no idea how happy that makes me. Of course, I saw you at Caroline's wedding. But I didn't know what to say to you, so I made sure to get lost in the crowd. I avoided you the entire evening and skipped the dinner."

Jason looked Reggie over and asked, "What about you, Reggie? What's that sign outside all about?"

"Yeah, that's not so good. I'm losing this place; can't keep up the payments to the bank."

"You own the place now?" Caroline asked.

"Yeah, I bought it from old man Samson eight years ago. But after a national hardware chain opened a super-store a few miles down on Route 52, I have had trouble keeping up my mortgage payments. I'm way behind, and the bank is foreclosing on the building."

Noah rolled up to them in his wheelchair and introduced himself to Reggie. "Hi. I'm Jason's dad. We never met, but Jason's mom and I have remarried and I'm living here in Bayville now. I'm retired, and Jason is heading my company. I overheard what you said. Has the bank told you they started the proceeding, or just that they intend to foreclose?"

"I got their letter two weeks ago. They want full payment of my loan plus arrears by the end of the month or they'll foreclose. But let's not spoil this happy reunion with my problems. I'm so happy to see these two together! I never met you, sir, but I'm also happy to see you and your son together. Of course I know Mrs. Housten, Jason's mom. The three of us used to hang out at her house all the time."

Kitty gave Reggie a big hug. "Great to see you, Reggie. Yes, the three of you were inseparable during high school. You were always my favorite among their friends." She gave Reggie another squeeze and continued. "As you just heard, Jason's dad and I are re-married and this is our granddaughter, Josephine, Jason's real daughter. We're one big family celebrating Christmas together for the first time."

Reggie looked admiringly at Josephine. "Oh my. You're a copy of your grandmother. You look so much like her that I suspected who you were the moment I saw you standing next to your mom. I have three daughters of my own. They are a little younger than you, but I hope to someday get you to meet them. Cindy, my eldest, was hoping to enter college next year, but that won't happen now."

That was right up Noah's alley. His old personality came back in a flash. "It's Christmas and I don't like to hear sad stories. You say you still own the building at this time?"

Reggie had no idea where Noah was going, but Caroline and Jason had a suspicion. Josephine beat them to it. "Granpa, you'll help, won't you?"

"Yes, I am thinking about it. Jason, you tell me you would like to own some real estate here in town. Main Street is a prime location. I suggest you and I bid on this building."

Reggie was taken aback by the offer but honesty made him say, "Sir, that is unbelievably generous of you, but the store is not profitable. I can't compete against that big super-store."

Small obstacles like that never deterred Noah. "Okay. Then we'll buy the buildings next door and build our own super-store. They'll have a hard time competing with you. A super-store with everything people need right here on Main Street, and locally owned to boot."

"Sir, I don't know how you knew the buildings next to us are for sale, but such a project would cost an unbelievable fortune."

Jason butted in, "Reggie, remember what I told you about my dad when we were in school? Well, he has not gotten any poorer since. Now that he is retired he needs a new hobby, and I think he has just found one. Say hello to your new partner."

It was all too much for Reggie. "Is this really happening? I have to be dreaming this! First I find out my two best friends from high school are back together. And now this. I can't believe it." He sat down and covered his eyes. He sat motionless for a moment. When he looked up he said, "I have to call my wife. She's got to come over right away and bring the girls along."

Kitty spoke up. "We're not going to celebrate this reunion of old friends here in a closed store. I still have dessert waiting for us at the house. Reggie, you remember where I live. Bring the family over so we can have a proper celebration."

An hour and a half later, Reggie, his wife, Wendy, and their three daughters pulled into the driveway. Walking up to the house brought back memories for Reggie. When he rang the doorbell, he remembered. The last time he rang this bell was exactly twenty-seven years ago.

Also by Harold J. Fischel
Taylor, The Journey Home ISBN:0692341811 /
ISBN 13:9780692341810
Anthony ISBN:1494851210 /
ISBN 13:9781494851217
Never Too Late ISBN:0692404694/
ISBN: 13:9780692404690

Reviews of Anthony

Reviewed By Jack Magnus for Readers' Favorite
Review Rating: 5 stars!

Anthony is a coming of age story written by Harold J. Fischel. Anthony is the child of Lieutenant General Bruce Walker and his mistress, Yuni. When Walker dies in an accident, he acknowledges Anthony as his son and provides for him and his mother. Yuni's medical bills quickly erode that inheritance, however, and she is forced to declare bankruptcy and move into a NYC Housing Authority project. When we first meet Anthony, he's trying desperately to persuade his mother to let him bring Zorbo, his dog, with them to the new apartment where dogs are not allowed. One of the movers who knows the manager of the building intercedes, and Anthony is allowed to keep his best friend. The new neighborhood is challenging for the young boy, but new friends, caring adults and the efforts of the coach at the YMCA make the transition a lot easier.

Harold J. Fischel's coming of age story, Anthony, is inspiring and heartwarming. Anthony's life is turned upside down by his mother's illness, but the adults he comes in contact with as he grows up help make his life story a triumphant one. Yuni's friend, Aunt Rita, is a marvelous character as are Kay and her parents. Anthony's progression from a withdrawn, small and chubby kid into a confident, caring and ethical young man is wonderful to watch. Fischel's writing style is accomplished and smooth, and I quickly became immersed in this athletic and ethical story of triumph over adversity. Anthony is a marvelous book and is highly recommended reading.

Reviewed By Lorena Sanqui for Readers' Favorite

Review Rating: 4 stars.

Anthony lost his dad to an accident at a young age, and then lost his mom, Yuni, to cancer when he was in high school. Yuni's best friend, Rita, took Anthony in and treated him like her own son until Rita's urges got the better of her and she entered into a sexual relationship with Anthony. Anthony was a willing participant, but being a minor and Rita's ward didn't go down well with the police and they sent Rita to jail. Now Anthony is back in college and he's having issues with getting into relationships. Luckily for him, Kay Goodman loves him very much and will not give up on him. Will Anthony and Kay get together and have a happy ending in Anthony by Harold J. Fischel.

Anthony by Harold J. Fischel is a wonderful coming of age novel. I loved the story of Anthony, but it didn't seem to follow one plot line. There were lots of smaller stories crammed in the book, although they all revolved around Anthony. It was okay but everything happened too fast; there was conflict after conflict so that it felt like there was no real climax and the ending seemed abrupt. On the other hand, I welcomed all the surprises and I loved all the characters. Anthony was resilient and strong, even when he was still a kid. Everything he experienced growing up only made him stronger, some of the things that happened to him even made me cry. Aunt Rita was a really nice person who just made some mistakes. Kay was persistent and supportive in all that Anthony does. All the supporting characters also played big roles in Anthony's success. Overall, a good book with great characters.

Reviewed By Melinda Hills for Readers' Favorite

I truly enjoyed the book and felt that it told a terrific story. You portrayed Anthony's younger years with warmth and compassion and provided him with many opportunities to rise above his circumstances. As he grew up and began the relationship with Rita, it was portrayed naturally and innocently in its own way and, again, provided opportunity for Anthony to grow, mature and understand himself. I really appreciate the way you allow Anthony to restrain himself in so many different situations and not 'go with the flow' – do what everyone else is doing because of peer pressure. It is also important later in the story as his daughter is intimidated by her fear of how others will react to her, so Anthony's experiences are a good background from which he can provide understanding and guidance.

The characters are realistic but I feel that they may be a bit too good. Jamal and Anthony are great friends and race is never an issue. Kay's parents are attractive, wealthy and very nice. At least Kay is more natural in that she never will forgive Sue Ellen. Even Anthony is easily convinced to return to school after his mother's death and after Rita is tried and convicted – he quickly accepts the guidance of others. This creates a rather shallow feeling about the characters although each of the scenes provides a worthwhile example or lesson even though they are wrapped up nicely before the next situation arises.

My main concern is that so much of the end of the story deals with Jackie and her 'coming out'. All of a sudden the story is no longer about Anthony – he happily accepted his daughter and went on his merry way while she continues to deal with her feelings and acceptance from her grandparents.

As you can see from the other ratings, I found the book to be very good overall, especially for young adults, but the ending needs to finish Anthony's story.

Reviewed By Mamta Madhavan for Readers' Favorite
Review Rating: 5 stars!

Anthony by Harold J. Fischel is a wonderful story of sadness, tragedy and hope. Anthony is the secret love child of a famous US General Bruce Walker and his mistress, Yuni. When Bruce Walker dies in a plane crash, though he has left a considerable amount of money in his will for his mistress and his son, the court rules against her and Yuni is forced to move into a tiny apartment in New York. Anthony becomes an easy target for the bullies who make his life miserable inside and outside the school, while Yuni is battling cancer. But things change for him slowly after an attack on him which makes him fight back. He grows to become tall and physically fit like his father. But as situations improve, another tragedy strikes. Now this time will Anthony be able to get through it?

The story evokes poignant feelings and it is wonderfully narrated. All the characters have important roles that have been portrayed well. Anthony's growing up and leaving behind a troubled childhood, to finally becoming a responsible husband and father has been developed well. His leaving behind the stigma of being an illegitimate son and then holding down an important job position is true to the times and resonates well with readers. The language is simple as it targets young adults. The story line is fascinating, which will make it difficult for readers to put the book down. On the whole, it is a very interesting book.

Reviewed By Katelyn Hensel for Readers' Favorite

Review Rating: 5 stars

Harold J. Fischel's book Anthony is as meaningful as it is simple. A simple story, with a normal plot, but the depth and the meaning within is so much more. To say that Anthony has had a rough life would be a major understatement. The product of an affair, his relationship with his father had always been strained, but then when his father dies, and his mother falls terminally ill, it's really like life is at an end. Neighborhood violence brings out a spark within Anthony that he didn't even know existed, and he starts to grow into a man - if not in mind, at least in body. His maturity, however, has a long way to go to match the newly adult body. It will take several encounters and shocking moments to get him to finally leave behind the doubts and pain of his childhood and become a true adult.

It's not often that I find a book that truly moves me, but Anthony may have just been it. Anthony is so real...such a realistic and poignant character. He is bitter, confused, sad, angry, and while his experience is not necessarily the norm of a typical young adult, you can easily relate to him. What a transformation. Anthony goes from a scared and weak child to a fierce, understanding, and competent young man. I loved seeing the way that other people had an effect on him. Usually you see characters change because of events that happen, but

Anthony really changed based on his perception of himself vs. the perception that others have of him. Fischel writes with skill and craftsmanship that is a joy to read. I would read anything else he has to offer in a heartbeat.

Reviews of Taylor, The Journey Home

R eviewed By Paula Tran for Readers' Favorite
Review Rating: 4 stars.

Taylor: The Journey Home by Harold J. Fischel describes a teenager and his transition into a young adult after a family financial crisis. Taylor, a junior in high school when the story first starts, lived a very extravagant lifestyle. He is the star of his school's football team, as well as a popular bachelor. He loves playing around with girls, moving on from one to the next faster than the change of weather, to the point where his mother is frustrated. However, things changed when Taylor found out that his family's business has crashed, and his world took a turn when his father committed suicide.

I think this novel is very well paced and extremely well written. The first few chapters were used to introduce us to Taylor, describing his playboy, care free attitude when it comes to anything. He is seen as reckless, making out with his girlfriend Phyllis, while knowing things can potentially get out of hand. However, I found it easy to relate to him, and I'm sure others will as well. Most people have experienced reckless teenage years and can relate to Taylor's problems and thought processes. I think this way of introducing Taylor is a good thing, because we get to know the character a little better. The plot is also well developed, a mix of emotional and suspenseful elements. However, for a high school student, Taylor seems too perfect. Sure, he has had ups and downs during his life, but his achievements suggest that he can be a little of a Mary Sue.

Reviews of Never Too Late

R eviewed By Anne-Marie Reynolds for Readers' Favorite

Review Rating 5 stars!

Never Too Late by Harold J Fischel tells a story of loves past and future. Sharleen and Clint used to be high school sweethearts, but one day his career on the field is destroyed by a shattered arm. By the time he recovers, Sharleen has moved on, and gone to Hollywood to become a starlet. Years later, they meet again at a school reunion. Both are now married, Clint to her best friend from high school and Sharleen to a notorious Mafia boss. Clint's business is failing, heading for bankruptcy, and his wife is sick. Can Sharleen help out on both counts? She has a strong connection to the Mafia that protects her, especially when she is arrested and locked up. But that connection cannot secure her bail. Her stepson, Freddy, steps in to help and is joined by Sharleen's cousins to help her escape from where she is being held prisoner. Join Sharleen on her adventures through life as we learn that no matter what life throws at you, it really is never too late to find what was meant for you.

Never Too Late by Harold J Fischel isn't quite the story you think it is going to be. It isn't as simple as meeting up after many years and falling in love all over again; life isn't that easy. Through all the to-ing and fro-ing, the arrests, the terror of being held at knife point, Sharleen still has so much to give and give she does. The underlying message here is that it isn't too late to find true love and happiness, and Mr Fischel has demonstrated that perfectly in this novel. The storyline itself was well thought out and written in such a way that I read it in one sitting. A good book and well worth the time it took to read it.

Reviewed By Julia Schemmer for Readers' Favorite

Review Rating: 5 stars

A rekindled love is a beautiful thing, but what happens when your lover has already found someone else? For the characters of Never Too Late by author Harold J. Fischel, this is exactly what occurs. Meet Clint and Sharleen, two star-crossed lovers whose different ambitions forced them to part to their own separate galaxies. When they are destined to cross paths again, this time it's a bit more complicated. Both are married; Sharleen to a mafia boss and Clint to her best friend. Can you say awkward? When trouble strikes for Sharleen, it'll take unfathomable courage and the help of her friends to get her through. Will Sharleen come out victorious and survive the odds, or has her time come? An inspiring tale of bravery, resiliency, and adventure; you do not want to miss out on this read!

My favorite books are not only the books that will leave me reading at 1 a.m. because I'm hopelessly drawn in, but ones that bring attention to pressing social issues. Luckily for me, Never Too Late by Harold J. Fischel fits both descriptions. Not only is the book a romance and an adventurous tale, but Fischel uses the power of his words to draw attention to issues that are commonly ignored, such as human trafficking and the existence of mafias. Through this book, I gained a new perspective on these issues due to his relatable characters that put a mental image on the issue. This book was truly a treasure to read, and I give it my highest recommendation.

Reviewed By Cheryl E. Rodriguez for Readers' Favorite

Review Rating: 4 Stars

Never Too Late by Harold J. Fischel is an action packed romantic drama. Frederick High's class reunion begins a chain reaction in the lives of the once golden couple, Sharleen and Clint. They were high school sweethearts, but their romance ends soon after high school. Clint leaves to play baseball for the Dodgers and Sharleen heads for Hollywood to become a star. Clint gets injured, moves home, and takes over the family restaurant. Believe it or not, Clint has married Jada, Sharleen's childhood best friend. Meanwhile, Sharleen becomes the wife of a Mafia boss, Giovanni Fuentes. Sharleen's husband is a jealous, domineering man; he keeps Sharleen well protected and on a tight leash. However, Sharleen is a good hearted woman, who is always willing to give a helping hand to those in need. When Clint's life begins to unravel financially, Sharleen secretly secures a loan for him. This begins a series of events that unites Sharleen, Clint and Jada into a three-stranded cord that is not easily broken. Sharleen believes that fate has brought them together. "Never too late" becomes a driving force to guide them.

Harold J. Fischel's Never Too Late proves the bonds of friendship, family and love. But hold on, it is not your normal romantic tale. It is fast paced; the short chapters keep the action moving, resulting in a captivating read. Anything and everything is thrown into the melting pot of conflict in this narrative - drug addiction, racial discrimination, cancer, Mafia hits and international sex trafficking. Characters are multiracial and Fischel highlights and portrays their different heritages throughout the story. The characters range from the self-righteous Italian mob to the traditional and numinous ways of Native American Indians. The heroine is strong, charitable and a romantic at heart, but believes that she has bad luck. The hero is masculine, yet at times vulnerable. These traits make the couple magnets for the down and out, causing their lives to intersect with many. However, the supporting cast of characters propels the action. The plot is a blend of romantic love and vendettas, benevolence and hatred, fear and faith, hope and despair.

Reviewed By Melinda Hills for Readers' Favorite

Review Rating: 4 Stars

It is 'never too late' to make up for past mistakes and that is exactly what drives Harold J. Fischel's novel by the same title. High school sweethearts Clint and Sharleen went their separate ways after graduation, but a class reunion brings them back together in an unexpected way. Clint is tapped out on financing for his restaurant, partially due to medical expenses for his wife, Jada. Sharleen has married a Mafia boss and has plenty of money at her disposal so she secretly backs a new loan for Clint. Jealousy and old-world mentality put both Clint and Sharleen in harm's way, so they flee to the safety of the reservation where Sharleen was brought up. Together, they establish a restaurant in Bermuda where they encounter a number of different people who have special needs of their own. Clint and Sharleen try to help everyone, even when it puts them in danger. Can their love see them through or will the hardships of the world ruin their chance at love?

Never Too Late is an exciting story about hope, forgiveness and second chances. Harold J. Fischel presents a variety of social problems through the actions of the outstanding characters and demonstrates that love and understanding can go a long way in making the world a better place. Vivid descriptions of places and people, as well as exciting action and thought provoking dialogue, keep you turning the pages, anxious to see what happens next. Never Too Late is an entertaining and engrossing story that makes you alternately hold your breath and cheer as Clint and Sharleen navigate the issues that plague them.

Extra comment: Your concept is excellent, however, and your treatment of the social issues you bring up is thought provoking.

Reviewed By Roy T. James for Readers' Favorite

Review Rating: 5 Stars

Never Too Late by Harold J. Fischel begins with Clint Crawley, who happens to bump into his old friends at a recent reunion and is shocked by the news of an impending financial disaster, finding his business threatened by banks. One of those friends, an old flame from his high school days, Sharleen, uses her connections with the underworld in helping him. Clint's wife dies, he meets Sharleen off and on to her husband's annoyance, and finally, they decide to move together to start a new life in Bermuda. There they 'continue to be a magnet for people with strange stories,' like Ana with a disadvantaged and mentally challenged young man, Mike, or Nina, a woman rescued from a local modeling agency which actually is involved with human trafficking.

Never Too Late by Harold J. Fischel is many novels compressed into one. Quite a few of the characters, seen to be part of Sharleen's life, can very well have an independent existence. Sharleen interacts with a variety of people from different walks of life, and in each instance the association leads to desirable inputs from her as well as happy reactions from them, establishing her strong character. With a narration that is deft and absorbing and a plot that is rich in its variety and content, I got the feeling that the eventful lives pictured in the novel finished too soon. This prompts me to say, 'It is always too early to finish Never Too Late.'